Dedalus European Classics
General Editor: Timothy Lane

CHASING
THE
DREAM

Liane de Pougy

CHASING
THE
DREAM

translated and with an introduction by
Graham Anderson

Dedalus

Supported using public funding by
**ARTS COUNCIL
ENGLAND**

Published in the UK by Dedalus Limited
24-26, St Judith's Lane, Sawtry, Cambs, PE28 5XE
email: info@dedalusbooks.com
www.dedalusbooks.com

ISBN printed book 978 1 912868 49 0
ISBN ebook 978 1 912868 56 8

Dedalus is distributed in the USA & Canada by SCB Distributors
15608 South New Century Drive, Gardena, CA 90248
email: info@scbdistributors.com web: www.scbdistributors.com

Dedalus is distributed in Australia by Peribo Pty Ltd
58, Beaumont Road, Mount Kuring-gai, N.S.W. 2080
email: info@peribo.com.au web: www.peribo.com.au

First published in France as *L'insaisissable* in 1898
First published by Dedalus in 2021

Translation copyright © Graham Anderson 2021

The right of Graham Anderson to be identified as the translator of this work
has been asserted by him in accordance with the Copyright, Designs and
Patents Act, 1988.

Printed & bound in the UK by Clays Elcograf S.p.A
Typeset by Marie Lane

A C.I.P. listing for this book is available on request.

The Translator

Graham Anderson was born in London. After reading French and Italian at Cambridge, he worked on the books pages of *City Limits* and reviewed fiction for *The Independent* and *The Sunday Telegraph*. As a translator, he has developed versions of French plays, both classic and contemporary, for the NT and the Gate Theatre, with performances both here and in the USA. Publications include *The Figaro Plays* (Beaumarchais) and *A Flea in Her Ear* (Feydeau). For Dedalus he has translated *Sappho* by Alphonse Daudet, *Chasing the Dream* and *A Woman's Affair* by Liane de Pougy.

His own short fiction has won or been shortlisted for three literary prizes. He is married and lives in Oxfordshire.

Dedication to L'insaisissable

To the Author whom I like best, to the Writer who, without knowing it, was my master, to Jean Lorrain I dedicate these first attempts of a poor little doll's brain which he opened up to vast horizons and to the unknown.

I offer him my book in gratitude… and in memory… and in friendship… and also in mild defiance… knowing in advance that those who read it and enjoy it will say that it is not by me… and those who find it bad will spare me none of their malevolence…

And to each of them, for his trouble… I say: Thank you!

Liane de Pougy

Introduction

L'insaisissable (Chasing The Dream) is the first of a number of 'courtesan novels' written by a young woman, born Anne-Marie Chassaigne, who received her education in a convent school and left it, pregnant, at sixteen; and who, a year or two later, abandoned husband and child, ran away to Paris and changed her name to Liane de Pougy.

Liane was her own invention, de Pougy a borrowing from an aristocratic lover. It had not taken Liane long to progress from chorus dancer and part-time prostitute to *grande horizontale*. For if she was going to make a living by selling herself, she was determined to sell to the richest patrons and live in style. Born in 1869, she had become by the turn of the century one of the most fêted courtesans of the day. She was not the first to exploit her situation, or enhance her profile, by portraying a version of the lifestyle in fiction. Her friend and mentor, Valtesse de la Bigne, had published *Isola* in 1876 and it may be that Liane thought to emulate her in literary matters as well. Or possibly she found Zola's *Nana* (1880) to be insufficiently first-hand. What becomes clear, however, is that Liane de Pougy the writer was by no means an artificial or temporary construct. She published eight books in the ten years from 1898 to 1908. The first of them, *L'insaisissable*, was written in 1895/96 and could be considered as a kind of half-time report on her career to date.

It describes the journey of its central character, Josiane de Valneige, from unhappy provincial housewife to glamorous courtesan, a journey she hopes will also lead to true love. The novel falls into two parts. The first is an animated account of her many adventures, some gleeful, some despairing, with a variety of lovers, from bankers and politicians to journalists and actors. Finding that none of these liaisons has led to the true happiness she seeks, Josiane retires to the country, where she falls for an innocent and ardent young man. Their idyllic (and chaste) relationship nevertheless comes to a sad end; and it seems that true love is indeed *insaisissable*, ungraspable.

Although it is her first work, and not a lengthy one, and is written by an author in only her mid-twenties, *Chasing the Dream* already has distinctive qualities. It has the structure of an epistolary novel: Josiane de Valneige's adventures are told to an old flame in a series of letters, to which he occasionally replies. The episodic nature of this first section becomes an asset rather than a drawback: the reader, like the old flame, is left at the end of each letter thinking 'Whatever next?' And in the second section, the confessional nature of the letters allows Josiane to be both actor and commentator as the relationship unfolds.

Alongside her sure-footed management of the story, de Pougy gives her heroine a particularly winning voice. Josiane de Valneige is energetic, ambitious and enjoyably vain. She has an acute sense of her own worth as a demi-mondaine whilst acknowledging how superficial those values are. She is funny, reckless and vulnerable. When knocked down, she suffers, but never for long. She will try again; the quest is always worth the gamble. If the particular voice here is Josiane's, the spirit behind it is very much that of the author.

Liane de Pougy's subsequent works include *Le mauvais part: Myrrhille*, which takes a darker look at the life of a courtesan; *Idylle saphique*, her most significant novel, which fictionalises her real-life affair with a young American woman, Natalie Clifford Barney; and *Les sensations de Mlle de la Bringue*, in which the heroine, damaged by her life as a courtesan, is nevertheless able to retire to Brittany (where de Pougy kept a cottage) to reflect in safety on her experiences.

At the age of forty, to the surprise of all, Liane de Pougy married. Her husband was Georges Ghika, a minor Romanian prince, fifteen years her junior. The former (and long-divorced) Anne-Marie Pourpe, née Chassaigne, famous for being Liane de Pougy, became Princess Ghika. A further transformation was in store towards the end of her long life. The marriage lasted, not without upheavals, until Prince Ghika's death in 1944.

It was the death of her son in 1914 that prompted Liane de Pougy, perhaps in atonement for her past life, perhaps in search of consolation, to turn to religion. Marc Pourpe, born in 1887, had been brought up by his paternal grandparents in Suez, where he had learned to fly. He was killed in an air accident in the first months of the Great War. Years later, in 1928, a second significant event brought focus to the vague quest for a greater spiritual purpose. The Ghikas made a chance visit to a convent in Savoy: it turned out to be an asylum for disabled children. The plight of the inmates and the devoted care given by the nuns made such a deep impression on the former Liane de Pougy that she became their no less devoted sponsor for the rest of her life, donating money for improvements to the buildings and raising funds from her many wealthy contacts.

As war loomed towards the end of the 1930s, the Ghikas moved to Lausanne in Switzerland, and there, after her husband's death, Liane de Pougy, befriended and counselled by Father Rzewuski, a Dominican priest, became a tertiary of the order of Saint Dominic.

Liane de Pougy died in 1950, aged 81, as Sister Anne-Marie de la Pénitence, and was buried in the grounds of the asylum of Sainte-Agnès which she had so long supported and which had become her spiritual home.

Liane de Pougy kept a diary between the wars, from 1919 to 1941, which was published posthumously in 1977 as *Mes cahiers bleus*. Diana Athill published an English translation, *My Blue Notebooks*, in 1979.

Idylle saphique (A Woman's Affair), Liane de Pougy's major work, is now available from Dedalus Books, who also publish Jean Lorrain's best known novel, *Monsieur de Phocas*.

I

The clock chimed two in the afternoon.

In the dressing room, warm and closeted, with its floating silks and the winter sun gleaming on its white lacquered furniture, Josiane de Valneige, lying full length on a chaise longue in the idle disorder of her negligee, ran her lips slowly round the rim of a small Meissen cup.

The angelic Gérard entered the room.

'The angelic Gérard' they all called her, this short, round woman, who had earned a fame of her own in the wider fame of her very beautiful mistress. And the name, in a phrase, said everything about her role in the house, explained the whole household itself. For did it not reveal that the woman who bore it with such dedication was, according to need, both servant and trusted friend, counsellor and accomplice, a guardian angel at times?

And when Mme de Valneige exclaimed: 'Oh, Gérard my angel, I am so out of sorts today!', this woman could respond in a manner all her own, affectionate yet with the sort of pleasing dignity that commanded respect, which made the angelic Gérard resemble some beloved family nurse of the kind Shakespeare gives his Juliet.

Mme de Valneige had gradually raised herself on one elbow. With her free hand she was languidly arranging her startling blonde hair, and in her blue eyes there seemed to shiver the traces of a dream.

'Gérard my angel... oh, no papers, no letters... don't bring me anything today... I don't want to hear anyone's news, I don't want to read a word... or even speak one... pass me my mirror.'

'Madame will change her mind. It's a surprise. Guess.'

'No, not this early in the day.'

'M. Leblois.'

'Jean!'

'He is here. He's waiting.'

'Oh! Send him in!'

Then, a moment later: 'Gérard my angel, take that picture of M. de Normande down from the mantelpiece... I don't know why it's there... it's not a good idea to mix the present with all those old memories Jean brings to mind.'

'Do you still love him, then?'

'Love him? Good Lord, no. That would be far too straightforward and sweet. Just a thought that comes to a woman's mind... quick then, Gérard, off you go.'

And Josiane sat up, knees raised under the light material, hands clasped round them. Her deep blue eyes unblinking, her face grave, she was a study in contemplation. And nothing is prettier or more rare than the spectacle of a woman lost in thought.

Amazing! Jean Leblois was outside! Could he really be about to appear, Jean, whom she had not seen for five years? It was true she had lost track of plenty of others over her career; she even congratulated herself on the fact and would declare herself extremely content never to see them again. But this man, for her, had special significance.

He had been the first: her first lover in a marriage that had become all too dull, the man who, at a time when she was the wife of a small-holder from the Touraine, on the slopes of Chinon, had taken her in adultery and kindled its full flowering.

Not that she expended much emotion – it already seemed so distant – on the memory of a provincial romance that was really a romance of the imagination. But all the same, this was the man with whom she had escaped, leaving behind everything. He was the one who enabled – precipitated – the break-up of a bourgeois existence too burdensome for an impatient twenty-year-old to bear, her flight into love and recklessness, her freedom, and then… all that followed. And if it was only to provide herself with an excuse, she was determined not to let this one be forgotten.

With a confident stride, his unclouded face wearing the smile of a friend, Jean Leblois came towards her.

She looked at him with curiosity and noticed that he was going grey.

A woman does not like to see a man she has had acquiring his grey hairs in a life beyond hers. It is as if he has done her some wrong in allowing himself to be used and tired out by another woman.

And straight away she said to him, having made him sit beside her and having retained in her own for a moment the hand he offered: 'My dear Jean, it is such a pleasure to meet again… tell me all your woes.'

'Woes? But I don't have any woes. I am now the most peaceful and naturally happy of fellows… oh, my poor Josiane, how I loved you…! It wasn't Josiane de Valneige in those days, it was Louise, little Mme Aubertin, a woman you'd have given the earth for… just as you gave me heaven back… I still have a letter where you said I was the man you used to dream about in convent school… and then, when we ran away to Paris, you in your brown dress, your little nose quivering in this new air, your eyes and your mouth drinking it in, the hôtel Malmaison in rue Lafitte, and our passionate love… or mine anyway.'

'Oh, don't think like that, Jean… I did love you…'

'In your way.'

Josiane was silent for a moment. Then, slowly, she said: 'Is it my fault if I didn't love you more…? All I wanted was to love you, yes, truly, I promise you… and all I want still is to be able to love you… but you now, tell me some more about yourself.'

'Me, my dear friend…? After all those long voyages my parents sent me on to break up our relationship, that was it with passion for me… I'm a married man, a father with a family to keep! For you I am now your devoted friend, who has come to visit you in the nicest sort of way. I can come without any danger.'

'Oh, do you think so?' Josaine said, a flash of coquetry springing to the defence of her womanly graces. But then, almost at once: 'Yes, my dear Jean, you are right. You took it into your head to pay me this visit and I am very thankful; thankful above all for your belief that I would still be pleased to have your friendship. I want to remain, in your eyes, the woman you knew and who had much that is good in her, whatever other people may believe.'

For in this unexpected situation, in this intimacy, Josiane found herself experiencing something both charming and delightful.

To know a man as a friend, a mere and simple friend, such a rarity!

It made her feel a different person, lending a new perspective that seemed both a pleasure and a benefit.

And to be discussing friendship, here, like this, in the dressing room of Josiane de Valneige, well, what a challenge to the public record!

When Jean Leblois had given a full account of his activities since those days up to his present life – which was in truth no more banal than anyone else's (he kept a protective eye on his land, wife and sons, hunted, read books in a fine house a short distance from Tours) – he concluded his recital with the sudden enquiry: 'But what about you, Josiane? Here you are, looking just as beautiful, in fact more beautiful than ever, but all the rest of it…? Tell me how you've been.'

'My life is simple enough, and very complicated. You say your days of passion are over: not so for me. You are in port, I am on the open sea!'

'But happy, at least?'

'Do we ever know…! Yes, yes, I do know: deep down, I am not happy.'

A sigh escaped her, and at the same time a sudden sadness spread across that exquisite oval face.

'Does that surprise you? How can a woman like me not be happy? And you think of this life I lead where the smallest whim is gratified. Alas…! Your eyes see this grand building in the rue de Prony, luxurious things all around me, luxuries I take for granted without wondering for a minute what they are for, where they come from, and you think: it can't be so, impossible, ridiculous! Josiane de Valneige, recognised as the bestower of supreme joys, incapable of finding any happiness of her own! Ah, what was the point of coming this far, of being what I am, for the end result to be this!

'Yes, a courtesan, my dear, a great courtesan, if there's any pleasure to you and credit to me in my saying it; and deep down less joyful, less enviable than the meanest of girls who come here delivering my feathered hats.'

And in her tone could be heard something both grieving and strangely sincere.

'In that case,' Jean said, 'speak out! Be open with me. What is wrong, my poor dear friend? If you are ever to be frank and trusting, you must be so with me.'

'No, no… men do not understand these things, and though I may have given some of them cause to weep, I have no desire to give you cause to laugh.'

There was a silence, during which Jean watched her closely. Then more quietly, with a note of regret in her voice, an instrument she could make resonate at her bidding, she continued: 'All the same, it would be good to tell it all to someone, a person who would understand, like you… to open my heart and ease the burden that stifles it.

'My heart, yes, and so many people believe there is no such thing. In the first place, a woman like Josiane, how can she have one, why must she have one? What a fanciful claim that would be, completely at odds with her behaviour, her way of life. Out of the question!

'Well, my friend, she does, a real heart, and a big one, and she knows it for certain from the way the things that are missing from her life bring her so much pain... so many things!'

'Keep talking, keep talking! Now we're getting to it!'

'Very well. But not like this. I have too much to say, I have seen so much... and one has one's modesty. In fact it's rather delightful to feel one has such feelings.

'I know what: Jean, dear Jean, I have never done anything for you, but here's my idea. I will write to you, regularly, yes, and lengthily too, on my crested notepaper with its de Valneige motto, "Where people catch a glimpse of heaven".'

She was pleased and excited by her idea. Naturally, if she had been a writer of no talent the thought would never have occurred to her. But she enjoyed a reputation for intelligence, culture and style, which had from the outset set her apart and which, even in the whirlwind of Paris, rather gratified the former pupil of the Sisters of Saint Agatha.

And then, to write in this way, to her first lover, about everything she had experienced with the others, certainly was no ordinary thing to do. But there was more to it than that: a moment had come for her when she sensed both the need to reach out and the release that might come from exploring her own story.

Starting from now, she understood, she was going to settle

accounts with her whole past life.

'So it is agreed, dear Jean,' she went on. 'You accept my proposition. Will there be jealousy at home? May I write to you as often as I like?'

And Jean gave her the address of a little place where they would keep for him the promised letters, letters that would present themselves as if at a confessional, and in which Josiane would share with him not just everything she had felt, had experienced in her past, but whatever might arise in the future.

'But will you write back to me,' she asked, 'from time to time anyway? I don't want to find myself soliloquising to the despatch bag of a rural postman! Tell me off, philosophise at me like a good stick-in-the-mud provincial, yes indeed, that will be fun; and feel sorry for me too when necessary.'

He promised, enchanted by his good fortune.

They talked on for a long time. They were like two friends making plans for a journey together.

And when Jean Leblois took his leave, he wished, in his mind's eye, he could already be ripping open the first envelope, while Josiane's gaze stole softly towards a little Meissen ink-stand that was waiting to one side, among the many trinkets...

'Madame,' the angelic Gérard announced when Josiane was alone once more, 'I forgot that M. de Normande sent to say that he would meet you this afternoon in the Bois de Boulogne.'

'Oh, for goodness's sake, as if I was interested in that, dear Gérard. Tell Brunet not to harness the coupé. And Mlle Alphonsine was meant to be bringing round the design for my trousers: send her away. I shall not be going out... I'm not in to anyone.'

Chasing the Dream

And stretching out once more on the chaise longue, Josiane de Valneige sank into her memories.

II

Josiane de Valneige to Jean Leblois

Shall I tell you, my dear friend, that when you abandoned me I expected to suffer immense distress? It is very comforting to believe oneself beyond consolation.

Unfortunately, I was not. For a week I remained in our little furnished lodgings, hounded by offers of forgiveness from M. Aubertin (who has shown no signs of life since), taking devotedly to our bed each night, reliving our existence as lovers newly arrived in Paris...

And then one fine morning, or evil one if you prefer, I realised nothing could be further from the truth. With some bewilderment, I understood that breaking the great taboo, which I had so longed to do, had left me little more satisfied with my fate than before.

You had had me, but how, and why? To an imbecile, and to preserve my own dignity, I would say: out of love. But you know, my dear Jean, that I was just an impossibly curious young woman, excited by the energy coursing through her bird's brain, her heart, her nerves, her body.

My husband would plod peaceably up and down his rows of vines, while I sat in my cheaply-covered blue armchair, mind adrift, eyes closed, a book abandoned at my feet.

Ah, what a narrow, stifling life! You can wither and die while all the time you feel inside you an unstoppable force is urging you on, a flame is burning you up.

What appalling torture!

First it's a feeling of contempt for everything around you, then hatred and finally something cracks, everything collapses inside. Rational thought does no good, not even fear holds you back. You go, you go, in the grip of this demon that whispers mad things in your ear, and without quite knowing how, you find yourself one day clasped in a lover's arms.

So don't be surprised at what happened after you. Whatever sort of creature I was when you took me, so I remained, or very nearly, when you left me. We had some good moments, but, don't take offence, hardly on the grand scale. And whatever made me give myself to you gave me to others: the constant search for pleasure's pinnacle, a burning thirst to drink from every cup, a yearning for excitement, glamour, domination.

In that little apartment where I wept over you, it was like being at home in the Touraine. The walls were bearing down on me, then suddenly, the roof, as if by a miracle, lifted and my dreams joyfully took flight like great birds.

To be something, to be someone, in that teeming Paris, to be a woman there, a real woman in the full understanding of the word: the power of that desire! And I sensed I had it in me, the necessary stuff, I sensed I was capable of knowing it all, of embellishing it… of being that woman!

Your old uncle Leblois showed me great kindness. When he saw I was utterly determined not to go back to my husband and to break away from my family entirely, and that I had neither money nor means of support, he came to my assistance of his own free will, with no speeches or strings attached.

I was therefore fairly secure for the immediate future (which doesn't excuse you for leaving me in such straits), but in truth I didn't greatly care. For me, money is not important, it doesn't exist. I have always managed to come by it, I always will… don't let's speak of it.

What a strange position a woman is in who wants nothing better than to… and who is on the lookout!

If you want my honest opinion, it is very enjoyable, especially when one does things properly. Besides, to my way of thinking it is unimaginable to do otherwise, and it is certainly a trait that has been my saving grace, as it will always be the saving of any woman even when her star is fading.

Oh, living in this permanent state of eager expectation, telling yourself life lies before you like an open field, where you may gather flowers, sniff the air, harvest the whole world for your own, without troubling about anything else! What sort of man will be the next to come along? What will love's ins and outs hold for you this time, or rather all the business that passes for love?

This is happiness as a guessing game.

Other people prefer it efficiently drawn up and guaranteed like an invoice or contract. But chance is not an enemy to me, I believe it arranges everything kindly and I walk with my eyes fixed on my lucky star. It can't be helped, my dear, it's the way one is born.

At any rate, I was convinced this star would not leave me languishing and that, an excellent state to be in, every sort of happiness was my due.

Come now, in all conscience, was I not deserving?

Think back. I was altogether charming, if I am now adorably worse: the look in my eyes, the clearness of my brow, and as for my mouth…!

Although I could be impetuous at times, my caresses had the touch of velvet. Although almost tall for a woman, I have a talent for making myself small, and in the corset of a man's hands my waist is as slender as that of a child.

I have an instinct for all that is graceful and supremely elegant. Arriving from the Touraine I awoke without transition as a Parisienne to the tips of my fingernails. A Parisienne on top, underneath and inside, and is that not exactly what they call the art of being a woman! Without taking a single lesson, I had understood everything.

So there was nothing left to do but make up my mind and get started!

What happened to all of that? At the present time I am beautiful in a very different way: the beautiful Valneige whose portrait is seen in windows along every boulevard next to that of the queen of England or the Pope. But in those days, the most beautiful thing about me lay concealed within: my faith in pleasure and kisses!

III

To the Same

One thing in this life of mine that I can always claim, dear friend, is that I got off to a flying start.

Others vegetate but I reached my goal right away.

Gaston was perfect, with his father's fortune. It allowed him to love a woman like me, who was to be so magnificently spendthrift, and to have his own racing stable, blue cap and orange sleeves, that never brought him in a penny.

Not for a moment did Gaston imagine I would settle for anything less than the very finest lifestyle. His self-respect would in any case not have wanted it otherwise, and my house was furnished like something out of a fairy tale.

Between Lardissen the interior decorator, Rousset the

fashion designer and Massabien the purveyor of linens, my hours were truly spun with silk and gold. And it was not merely for the pleasure of opening the windows and throwing in handfuls of the precious metal – despised only by those who don't know how to use it – it was also with the intention of proving my superiority and my taste.

One of the most satisfying moments for any woman is when she gives herself entirely to the task of making herself beautiful, the focus of esteem, envy, love. Throughout the organising of all this – with such amusing little details! – the old penny-pincher who hopes you will cover everything in his crocodile skins, the angelic Gérard who turned up to offer her services as a manicurist and almost immediately made herself an indispensable member of the household, the piano teacher who guarantees you a competent polka in three lessons, the man who deals in King Charles spaniels, the whole band of fakes and swindlers who want to sell you their services – I felt like a theatre director overseeing his set and his production ahead of a major premiere.

My personal premiere took place at Auteuil, at the races.

'Now that's a pretty woman!'

'Who is she?'

'No one knows her.'

Ah, the thrill of joy when one becomes a Paris event! To feel so much curiosity and desire circling round you. To know you are at the admiring centre of life's greatest concentration of elegance, wealth, happiness. And to have on you too the eyes of women who know what's what and are judging you, and of the ones who are about to be eclipsed by you and can't help revealing their fear!

Sitting on my chair, alone, for several minutes I drank in the giddy excitement of it all. So this was it. Paris. Here it was before my eyes, all around me, I could feel it rumble, roil, shudder in all its beauty and terror, and I was part of it.

I shall never forget that first minute when I came into my possession and I must have looked quite radiant because when Gaston, a few moments later, came to join me as the bell rang and the noise of the crowds rose on all sides for the start of the racing, he said to me: 'My dear, you have caused a sensation, you are marvellous, they love you.'

'So, I hope you are pleased.'

'And very proud to show them you are with me… ah, what a happy accident it was to leave the Jockey Club at exactly the right moment to meet you going into the Old England.'

A little later we took a stroll through the bar; he even gave me his arm for a while. He introduced me to some of his friends, and your little Mme Aubertin found herself accepting the ovation of a really top-class field, as they liked to say then.

I was wearing a costume in the armorial colours of the stable and there wasn't a single person in that circle who wasn't both titled and a notable person of influence. And it was in the course of that afternoon, as it happens, that I was christened.

Perhaps you have wondered about the name I use, Valneige. It's very simple: I have the honour of being named after a horse.

Valneige! Valneige!! By happy fortune the winner of the day, the only one of Gaston's horses that ever did anything! To commemorate such an unforgettable event and to make sure no one should remain in ignorance of it, Valneige, it was agreed, should become my nom de guerre, a very decorative name too, and without needing further persuasion, Beauty took the name of the Beast.

That moment was certainly the happiest – on the outside – of my life. It was the honeymoon period of my launch into society, of champagne and sleepless nights.

A cast-iron stomach, a frame that could withstand anything: I was seen everywhere, at any hour of day or night. I was the epitome of the women of whom one asks, 'How does she do it?' How? I simply let myself go, sustained by a burning fever worthy of the unfortunate Lady of the Camellias.

From the very first minute there was not a single false step between Gaston and me: he knew what it was that attracted me, what I was looking for out of life, and he gave it to me, I have to say, in full knowledge and like a perfect gentleman.

We went to all the little theatres, concerts in out-of-the-way places, all-night restaurants, cabarets in Les Halles, buffet suppers in Montmartre: I saw it all, with its attendant company of black-suited, gardenia-buttonholed types. And what Gaston particularly enjoyed was the originality of having to educate his mistress in all of this, a woman, however, who proved herself to be completely unprejudiced. He would say, laughing, that it was like being one of those newly married husbands who find great amusement in depraving their wives.

I was an excellent pupil, my friend, believe me.

None of which implies that I ever gave Gaston anything to reproach me for.

I restrained myself, however impossible and pointless that may seem.

Not that opportunities were lacking. His friends, to start

with: there was a whole little collection of them to choose from. The nicest of all was Preilly, the lover of Mme de G***, a woman who wanted, it appeared, to get to know me by any means available. Preilly, I had him afterwards... why not? And I still remember how furious he was when, wishing to embrace him (embracing, my dear, please note, has nothing in common with kissing) I had the temerity to disturb his parting.

On many evenings I received at home. One of my entertainments was even described in Le Gaulois and le Figaro.

As for love, nothing, or almost nothing!

But the biggest struggles I had to face were with women. You can have no idea how determined they were to make me cheat on Gaston! I used to meet frequently with several who were constantly in the public eye, the cream of the milk: Louise Martin, Mme de Darcy, Suzanne de Cologne, Mathilde de Courcelles, and then there were some of the little boulevard actresses: Rose Lafeuille with her chap, a theatre critic, Laure Chiné and her half-baked stockbroker, Jeannette Lévy with her companion Mastic. Well, all of these women, without exception, acted as stimulants, drove me on.

I shall not even tell you the name of the woman who arrived one day bearing offers from a rich Brazilian general with a diamond-studded cigar-holder. Even the angelic Gérard, one morning when I was in the bath, tried to interest me in one of her protégés, a Belgian who wouldn't have interfered with my life and simply wanted to be on my list.

It would have been ridiculous to get angry at all of this, and inappropriate; I simply laughed at it and took note.

I have always had a kind of loyalty that goes down very well in this field of activity. Although I know all there is to know about how passions operate, even then, when one finds oneself unusually well placed, I believe one should know how to behave correctly. It is a form of commercial honesty.

In any case, why would I have wanted to cheat on Gaston?

He was a very handsome fellow, ready for anything, and knew how to make a woman happy, several women even... I owe him that tribute, along with a little gratitude for everything that, as a man of the world, he did for me.

Now he is married, like you, my friend, but I am sure that he too treasures happy memories of our liaison.

It lasted several months, it could have lasted many more.

But at this point we encounter what must be considered the flaw in my character, or if you will, the excuse for it and the best part of me.

I had 'arrived', as they say, all along the line, my every need supplied, my public face that of a woman having the time of her life, thrilled by the sheer allure of it all, and yet something was missing. The further I advanced and the more material comfort I acquired, the more I became aware of an empty space inside.

'What's wrong, my dear?' Gaston asked. 'Several times now I seem to have caught a pensive look in your eye... are you bored...? Is there something you want?'

'No, I assure you, everything is fine.'

On another occasion he said to me: 'I bet I know... I've guessed.'

'What?'

'Why you've come over all dreamy... when a woman begins to day-dream like that... come on, be open about it at least... tell me everything: it's a crush, you've developed a little crush on someone... who is it?'

I needn't tell you he didn't believe a word he was saying. But he was closer to the truth than he thought. I was in love... yes, I was! Only what I was in love with was love itself!

Yes, agreed, I had everything a woman like me can wish for; some even said, more than she deserves. Nevertheless, deep down inside, I realised I was very unhappy. How could I have been so silly? Did you ever see such a creature? Well, yes, you have seen one, because everything I have just set down is true, is sincere.

To be loved is hardly an accomplishment, it's nothing to be all that proud of; it happens to the plainest of women and in the most surprising of ways; to love is everything. And we would be very contemptible creatures if we thought otherwise.

To love someone, love someone, love someone!

All of a sudden I discovered this inner need just when I imagined I was perfectly content; and the most dangerous thing was that this need had nothing to latch on to, nowhere to go.

To love... but who was the man? Oh, if only I'd known! But no. I was burning with a fever that never went away, that couldn't be overcome, and whose cure was unknown.

I looked in Gaston's direction, I tried to kindle my imagination in his favour, I could even see detailed reasons why he deserved to be loved, but I felt nothing. The correctness of his conduct under the severest test, the kindness and decency of our behaviour with each other, the satisfaction he gave me, no, that was not it. And the less I loved Gaston, the more I felt how wonderful loving someone would be, how good, how comforting!

Chasing the Dream

So then I looked around me, casting an eye over the people I knew. I was dreaming about things that seemed far removed, when perhaps happiness already lay close at hand. Come along, which of these men might make me feel something and be worthy of receiving all the tenderness I felt I had in me? It was the tenderness – not to be scorned, I can assure you – of a woman who now grew misty-eyed in her box at the theatre whenever the orchestra struck up a wistful tune and who read up all the stories of lovers' suicides in the papers.

But in my circle, nothing, no one. And I consulted – don't mock – a clairvoyant in the rue des Martyrs.

'Shall I ever be able to love? Or find someone to love?'

I don't know if she was unusually far-sighted, but she was polite enough to tell me there was no doubt about it… I will love someone.

She also saw, examining my palm, the line of fortune. Fortune! I didn't care a jot about that just then, it was happiness I wanted. And who should I turn to for that? Where to seek relief from this undefinable disquiet – which was, I admit, a sensation I cherished?

Love, love, oh, I made it all the time. But how different it must feel when you love and your heart is in it!

The heart, yes, my friend; the unexpected protagonist in this sad state of affairs was my heart. And when I saw that I had one and that all it asked was to beat powerfully for a whole array of good things, everything suddenly altered within me.

For example, I would have experienced a definite sense of pain, previously, if anyone had told me Gaston would eventually break off with me. He did break off – oh, in the most gentlemanly fashion – and not only was I not for a second angry with him, I very nearly flung my arms round his neck.

He disappeared from my life one morning, leaving me well provided-for, mistress of my own future and, despite all I had learned, an innocent still in one matter, my heart.

And oh, how long was this virginity of mine to last? What did fate have in store for it?

You will not mind waiting a little to know the answer, my friend, and I have read too many novels not to write with perfect naturalness at this point: *To be continued next time*.

IV

To the Same

I had not yet acquired Gaston's successor when something happened that could have had serious consequences. It will give you a good idea of the state I was in at the time.

One evening, we had been dining at Madrid, round a table, with friends.

Ah, what a marvellous summer evening it was, my dear! People who don't look up at the Paris sky don't know what they're missing; it's unique.

Over our heads was a cloth of blue, with stars too numerous to count, and a cool breeze wafting through the chestnut trees.

I don't know if you are familiar with Madrid, in the Bois; it's a spot I like very much because you get the full bustle of street life at the same time as something quite intimate and hidden away. Over in one corner are the horses from our carriages, stamping their hooves, and voices calling to the coachmen, Ernest, Auguste, from the rue Blanche; but around all the noise and activity there's this mysterious greenery and a very soothing sense of calm.

Unfortunately for me, orchestras and bands are all the rage just now; they are everywhere; you can't drink or eat any more except to music. The appeal of the universal Exhibitions may have passed me by but one result of them at least has been to leave in their wake hordes of fiddlers of various descriptions forever buzzing round you like flies.

But I have nothing bad to say about the orchestra at Madrid. I even owe it a minor debt of gratitude for what nearly happened because of it. And look, even as I write I can see him again, my splendid gipsy violinist, erect there in his blue trousers and frogged scarlet tunic!

He stood slightly forward of the others, chin bent over his violin, in the pose of a god.

He made such a handsome sight, how could anyone have been unaffected? Never in my life have I seen a more profoundly expressive head: the dark hair swept back with masculine vigour, the features too, noble and sharply drawn as the light fell on his even complexion, had a forceful and bold character.

All this, however, was softened by the eyes and lips.

Big brown eyes, shimmering and changing like velvet, now staring, now melting into something like a caress; and the ardent red mouth, quivering, stretching, offering itself and showing, when it half-opened as if for a kiss, a glimpse of

34

dazzling white teeth.

And it was the sway his own music held over him that made his expressions change: he looked quite transported, intoxicated by the sounds he drew from that violin and the melodies he sent swirling over us.

Their voluptuousness, their agonies of love! Where did such depth of feeling come from? At times he seemed to leave his own body altogether, gazing up into the sky, the stars, seeking inspiration or perhaps refuge there. It was super-human, frightening, and not a single part of me remained unaffected.

Of course this was not the first time I'd been made aware of the strange charm, the kind of spell these people can cast. They have caused some well-known disturbances in Parisian life, and you will readily recall the case of Mlle P***, much discussed, the multi-millionaire's daughter who every evening rushed off to wherever they were playing, sat as close as humanly possible and was last to leave at the end, dragging herself away half-fainting…

For my part, I had never been 'hooked' like that. Why was it I couldn't resist on this particular evening? That violin so shook my nerves it very nearly stripped them bare. And that man literally had total control of me from his platform.

Oh, my goodness, they're wicked, and they recognise the signs! When they notice that somewhere in the audience the effect is working on some woman or other, they're not slow to pull the strings.

Mine, for me, played a waltz, and then another. A waltz, my dear, means nothing at all in the ordinary run of things. It sends a little tingling up our legs, sets off a little fizz of

35

pleasure in our brain, and that's all there is to it. You do a twirl, you point your toe, you dip your waist a little, nothing special has happened, it's just one more Waltz of the Roses.

But those sorts of waltzes, they're a whole world of their own. They contain everything: love even: all of it, before, during and after.

And the gipsy, from a distance, was keeping an eye on me. He made it clear it was me he was playing for, me alone, never shifting his gaze, swaying his body to the rhythm and he aimed, he fired, his notes straight between my shoulder blades… it felt as if he was coming nearer and nearer, he was going to play right in my ear.

For heaven's sake, one does not put a woman into this sort of state! Or rather, yes, one must do exactly that, and here's to the men who know how to keep her in it a good long time!

I was still shaking when a voice close to us said: 'Kindly don't forget… ladies… gentlemen…'

My gipsy was there holding out a plate on which a napkin had been folded in four, and giving his most gracious smile, he tossed the coins on it into the air.

When he stood in front of me, his brown eyes at once took on their lovely magical shadings of colour and, still holding the plate out, he was now murmuring something incomprehensible in their special soliciting manner.

And I gave him a twenty francs piece.

What a strange thing to do, giving twenty francs to a man!

He calmly went back to his place, as if nothing had happened, and picked up his instrument.

I too put the horrid interlude out of my mind; and while at all the tables nearby people were chattering and laughing loudly, I slipped back into my thoughts and, in spite of myself, focussed my full attention on my musician.

He had turned for my pleasure to music of a melancholy strain now. Conducting the others as he played, he drew from the orchestra harmonies of indescribable richness. And this after the waltzes! After the excitement, my dear, and the sensual whirlwind!

It was a song from their own country, slow, grave, swollen with sighs and tears, a love song, but of a kind unknown to Parisians like us.

It struck me like a blow to the heart. Yes, this time it was the heart that reacted.

I would have liked to sigh and weep also.

Oh, how far I was from my friends, far from my life, far from everything! I was in my gipsy's country, a beautiful country it must be if they created things like this and felt them too. I was in a state of rapture, and I wondered if fate had not led me to this spot tonight on purpose.

When the music stopped, something seemed to stop in me too.

I was torn apart inside, and yet overwhelmed by a feeling of infinite sweetness.

Oh, what a profound sense of languor, of tenderness, what a trembling in my soul! Don't laugh. After all, if the man could play like that, must he not have had something in his heart that moved him? Who knows, a lover, a fiancée left behind in his home country! Yes, to stir me like that in the very fibres of my being, he must know such emotions himself. And what he had just made me feel he could surely make me feel again, and go on doing so for ever.

For a long while I sat there, deep in thought, not really there at all, unaware of my surroundings. Then, strangely full of emotion, I looked round for him...

He had vanished!

As if in the power of some invisible force, I rose to my feet. Where was he?

I wanted to see him whatever it cost; I had to; I had a wild desire to speak to this man, to give him a kiss, to offer him all the brimming emotion he had filled my heart with, begging him at the same time not to leave me like this but to restore the life to and in fact take over my entire being.

I began to search for him, on the darker side of the garden, I looked behind the shrubbery and over by the stables.

Meanwhile, in his absence, the orchestra carried on playing. At last, at last, in a kind of arbour reserved for the serving staff, I caught sight of him...

Bent over a rickety table, illuminated by a candle stuck in a bottle, his handsome red tunic unbuttoned and hanging loose, he was – lumpishly, gluttonously – he was eating, and his thick fingers were scrabbling at a greasy paper packet and spilling fragments all over the place.

Oh, my friend! I tried to tell myself that even on the banks of the blue Danube it is normal to feel hungry and to eat, but it was a truly repulsive discovery.

I would have given anything not to have come upon my ideal, my god, almost my true-love in that posture, filling his face in such a horrible fashion...!

No, it was impossible. This was not the same man as a minute before... I was the hapless victim of a wicked deception...

A victim, indeed, of my heart, of my need to believe and to belong.

And while my gipsy, intent on the joys of the stomach, carried on chewing, uttering little grunts of animal satisfaction, I retired in good order.

My dear Jean, I can see your face from here as you read the tale of my mishap.

That poor Josiane, you are thinking, hasn't got enough to fill her time, and you are not entirely sure of the quality of my brain. Only someone with her mind a little askew could get carried away like that!

But what do you expect? You're going to have to resign yourself to hearing plenty more along similar lines. Besides, if I only told you stories of unadulterated happiness and occasions when everything went swimmingly, you wouldn't find it greatly entertaining.

I could tell you stories like my gipsy's by the dozen, every shift from hope to disappointment, from scaling the heights to coming down with a bump, that's my whole case history. I have a season ticket for the switchback!

You can see that today I take the cheerful view: it won't perhaps be that way all the time!

V

To the Same

It is not my intention, dear friend, to give you a list of names here.

I would not have the courage, and in any case there would be no pleasure in it.

What do they matter to you, the men I have had? And what do they matter to me? They were passers-by, and nothing is left of them but a few trinkets. Some of them had so small a part to play in my story that not even their names have stayed in my memory.

What I promised you is something more interesting: to put on stage the ones who were candidates in my quest for love, and describe what transpired.

Chasing the Dream

So let us leave in peace what I call the serious men, long-standing friends: the old senator whom I knew in the same way as the others and whose velvet skull-cap lived at my house; the magistrate, please your worship, who studied Madeleine Chamberon's trial papers on my chaise longue; that nice M. B*** who used to tell me all about his stock lists and ask my advice about setting up his daughters; old N*** from the Cosmopolitan Bank who squashed some of my fanciful ideas and simply told me, tapping my cheek: 'My child, you will never come to anything!'

Come to anything? Come to what, I ask you? Do I harbour some great ambition?

I don't dream of riches that will set everyone talking. I think all those châteaux in Seine-et-Oise are a joke!

My castle, if I have one, my dear, is a castle in Spain. It is where, one beautiful moonlit evening, love would enter in, or even one afternoon in bright sunlight.

So I am going to tell you about some of the situations which offered hope in my search for happiness, and how I felt about them. It is a trail strewn with misadventures and perhaps you will be touched by the fate of a woman who has done everything she can to find love in an age when it is claimed loving is no longer a thing anyone desires!

...Since I must dare tell you even the worst, I shall begin by telling you what I found attractive about little Duluc. It was his bad reputation.

Bad in terms of morality, which frankly bothered me very little, but excellent in terms of a particular kind of loving.

The whole of Paris knows little Duluc: he is the life and soul of all the clubs he belongs to, he is a star of the polo-playing set, he has single-handedly compromised the reputations of a hundred women, the best in society amongst them, he is the idol of both the smart set and the rakish; the little man is a real charmer.

He sports a stylish pencil moustache more elegantly than anyone you've seen, his eyes have a special twinkle, and his smile... oh, little Duluc's smile! You seize on it like an invitation to a party.

And indeed, that's what it is, an invitation; to love each other, to try it out, see where things might lead.

It must be acknowledged, alas, that we women are tempted to love a man largely for his potential faults, or even, let's say, between ourselves, his vices.

With little Duluc, it was said, one was embarrassed for choice!

Several of my women friends, or friends of my friends, had brief liaisons with him, for it seems that no one ever has one that counts, and the way they talked about him could make one truly envious.

'Little Duluc,' said Louise Martin, 'the way he talks to women, my dear, you've no idea...! There's no one else like him... it's like being lightly spanked with a riding crop... it's quite wonderful.'

'Ah, my dear!' murmured Suzanne de Cologne, 'a woman doesn't get bored in his company...! He's a true artist... until you've had this little fellow you haven't lived!'

Why then would I have denied myself a treat coming with such high recommendations? One evening little Duluc was brought to one of my dinner parties. Gallex the painter was there, an embassy attaché, Doctor Miron and some friends.

So, was the diminutive figure really as irresistible as all that; and if love were lacking, would I at least feel desire?

Well, there are no two ways about it, this Duluc is positively exhilarating. Written into his every gesture, every feature, his whole bearing is the message that this is a man who knows his way around, and there is only one expression that would describe my feelings…

And goodness me, it's too bad, I'll say it, I'm not sending you the impressions of an innocent maiden after all! Little Duluc, just the look of him is enough to be sure – some people are privileged in this way – he's the business!

After dinner, we had coffee served in the conservatory.

It's the place I like best in my whole house, a fantastic creation of plants and fabrics.

And also, I always feel especially attractive in that setting.

Little Duluc was very animated and eager to please, but he didn't need to be. We talked, we had music, Tibert made us laugh with his impersonations and sketches of Parisian life, and when at one point I found myself in my Venetian loggia, sitting on a divan beside little Duluc, he took my hands in his.

Well now, Jean, if anyone buried in that provincial fastness of yours – which is mine too as it happens – were to read this letter (anyone but you, that is), a letter describing an evening at Josiane de Valneige's, I'm sure their imagination would conjure up a very false picture!

An evening at the home of a woman like me must surely be, mustn't it, a scene of hilarity, silly behaviour, risqué manoeuvrings and general commotion with an orgy to finish! Well, things do not happen like that at all, the legend is dead, it's old hat.

43

Nowhere are people so well-behaved or observant of good manners, of what the English, I believe, call 'tone'. To put it plainly, this disordered, anything-goes lifestyle we are supposed to lead is punctiliously correct in every way and the strictest arbiter in questions of education, dignity and high style would find nothing to criticise.

Our after-dinner activities, then, proceeded in a manner that would satisfy the most fervent admirer of this noble quarter of Paris. There was even, if I remember rightly, a brief moment of boredom which was perfectly in tune with requirements.

I, however, was not in the least bored.

And I don't know how it came about, but towards eleven o'clock, when Gallex mentioned he might go out to 'have a little something' on the boulevards, when the attaché mentioned a 'do at the club' that sounded promising, and when the doctor rose to go and pay an urgent visit to his leading lady patient, there was something like a fire burning in my veins, I was positively happy to see them making ready to go, my temples were throbbing and I couldn't or didn't wish to control myself...

And little Duluc stayed behind.

He even found it all very natural.

The next day I was as happy as a lark.

You may guess what that means.

Time to read between the lines.

Oh, Jean! Conjure up in your mind all the things that can go on between two lovers carried away by passion! We were literally besotted with each other. He sent me into frenzies of excitement, the sort of physical obliteration of the senses that makes two people in reality only one and makes them seem like souls without bodies when they are not together.

It seemed to us, quite sincerely, that we couldn't ever be separate beings again. He was very proud of this success; I was shaken by it, and thrilled all the same.

We no longer went out. It was as if little Duluc had been erased from the boulevards. Ah, those lunches in our bedroom, followed by a wave of tiredness again, and a rest, so-called, which promptly tired us out still further!

In the evenings, we still stayed indoors, just the two of us; but the lights were on everywhere, and a festive air in the house as if I had been entertaining twenty guests; and it was just for us! For him...

'This evening,' little Duluc would frequently say, 'this evening, maybe, I'll take you to the theatre.'

'Yes, lovely.'

'Or else to the Folies Bergère, or the Eldorado. Or we'll just go out for a walk...'

'Fine, wherever you like.'

And do you know where we ended up, my dear? No further than the bedroom, a tea tray to hand and me in my dressing gown!

I did, however, have a visit from a woman friend who announced that she thought I looked a little pale.

'But it suits you very well,' she told me.

And she was right.

It had all been going on for three weeks by this time, three weeks of wildness and excess. I was completely shattered, I was begging for mercy, but in a state of absolute physical fulfilment.

'We love each other, don't we?' I would say, taking his head between my hands. 'You love me… I feel you love me… and I'm all yours too. What I'm feeling is something I've never felt before…'

He would placidly let me maunder on.

'And we shan't ever separate now, shall we, my little Duluc…? Do you feel the same…? Come on, you have to answer. Quick, tell me something kind and loving to give me pleasure.'

And he would light a cigarette! Whilst I was off in the land of dreams… yes, for sure, what I'd had was wonderful, I relished this amazing satiation of the senses as it deserved to be relished, but would there be nothing more?

How comforting it would be to feel a mutual sense of belonging, just to remain here, hand in hand, without saying a word or doing a thing…!

I imagined another form of happiness must follow in the wake of this brutish, near crazy passion. Some instinct drew me towards this other joy, which would be made out of ideas that haunted me, lovely ideas.

To be two people in love, to show a side of Josiane de Valneige no one suspected! And in addition, I was thinking what a triumph it would be if I was the one who succeeded in keeping my little Duluc when all my predecessors could not.

'Tell me,' I asked him one day, 'how exactly do you love me?'

'How can you possibly not know?'

'Yes, yes, I do know, of course I know… but on top of that, don't you feel just a trace of real affection for me…? I'd so much wish you to love me, the way I feel I'm going to love

46

you… with proper emotions, it would be so good.'

And I can still hear his reply.

'My dear Josiane, you are unlike anyone else… you're full of the maddest ideas!'

After that day, from the welcome my proposition received from him, it goes without saying, my friend, I clung to it all the more tenaciously.

Yes, he would love me… yes, I would contrive to force into his heart all the emotions that set mine racing!

But on one occasion he told me: 'Don't expect me for dinner tonight… I'll be staying on at the club…'

'Well, I'll come and fetch you!'

'Oh, don't do that.'

'Are you cross with me?'

'No, but it would look silly.'

Another time, he didn't tell me in advance; it was simpler.

When he returned, looking bored, it was very late. Can you picture such a scene, my friend, Josiane de Valneige in her bed, waiting?

To sum up, it didn't take me long to understand…

I had believed for a while that all this pleasure could turn into a wider fulfilment. Feeling in me the need for true affection, for a bit of blue, as the poets put it, I had imagined I could find it here… and my little Duluc, on his side, had simply come to the end of his repertoire and was in a state of repletion!

So the thing didn't drag on long after that.

What was the point in prolonging a situation that could no longer give me anything and which couldn't change?

He left me one night when there was a ball at the Opéra,

at which he set about sweeping a new woman off her feet. He left me, delighted by our whole experience and ready, he said, to put right any man who ever dared in his presence speak ill of Josiane de Valneige, who was a truly fine woman; and I, disappointed, I left him without anger but with a little sigh just for myself, which he would not have understood at all.

So much for having aspirations... that'll teach you, my girl!

VI

To the Same

I send you here, excellent confidant that you are, a few more pages and a little anecdote.

I have mentioned N***, of the Cosmopolitan Bank. This N*** was a good man: what he wanted from me was the simple satisfaction of being free to call on Josiane de Valneige, from time to time, to take tea and talk.

But it was through him that I came to know Martigny, another important financier.

Important financiers had their own special place in the lives of women like me; they do in everyone's lives, do they not?

But what marked out my Martigny as distinct from the

others was that he enjoyed the esteem of society in general.

His correctness in business matters was proverbial and his professional conduct widely admired.

God knows I'm no bourgeoise, my friend... perhaps I am not bourgeoise enough. But however much one might be... what shall I say?... a free spirit, when a sober-minded, honourable man takes an interest, it is always flattering to a woman.

There were other ways Martigny had of pleasing me, and the best was that he swore he loved me.

Where others would only have offered their station in life, the glamour of their wealth, their personal stylishness, this one would speak of true affection... and he was adorably jealous, of everything, of everyone...

Even of his secretary, a curly fair-haired young man who arrived at my house each morning to bring him the latest up-to-the-minute news, respectfully handing over little cards dense with figures.

Martigny's manner as he looked at them, it was wonderful! Yes, really, you'd think all those numbers written there were no concern of his, such trivialities meant nothing to him, what was the Stock Exchange to him, what was money?

'No,' he would murmur indifferently, '...I don't want to know any of this, I don't want to hear business talk.'

And to end it, he liked to quote a line we'd heard at the Théâtre-Français:

The time that's left shall all be for Zaïre!

Wasn't that charming?

The great financier's Zaïre couldn't get over it!

She being, you understand, a person who naively believed

a great financier must talk only of schemes and accounts, read only *The Financial Week*, go nowhere without a little gold pencil in his hand!

No, nothing of the sort with Martigny: he exuded disdain, a contempt unique among his kind for all such carryings-on, so thoroughly beneath one!

I found this quite simply magnificent.

At last I had met a gentleman, a rare bird, the phoenix of modern times.

'Is it right, then,' I said to him one day, 'that I'm the only one who exists for you?'

And although I could talk to him like this, I still addressed him as *vous*. It's a curious thing, there are some men it doesn't come naturally to call *tu*, even when we like them a great deal.

'If so,' I continued, 'did you know you are about to make me extremely proud and happy?'

'It is my one desire.'

'Is there anything keeping you in Paris?'

'Only you. Do I have any other occupation or concern but to make myself agreeable?'

'Well, in that case, let's go away, if you're willing, for a few days to… to the seaside…'

'What…? Well, gladly: just as long as it takes to rent a villa and have it arranged as befits you.'

Oh, my friend, the idea of leaving Paris for a while, going to some peaceful, little-known spot, with a man who appreciated me, who in all the universe had eyes only for me, wanted only me, it was a dream! Was the impossible by chance going to come true this time? Might I at last be permitted to know a little true emotion and intimacy?

'When do we leave?'

'Straight away, of course! Who needs a villa to be happy?'

With a good and tender smile, Martigny put me right, and it was agreed we would take flight on the following day.

I was impatient, I was filled with joy!

The next day, at the appointed time, I was waiting at the station.

We were due to meet under the clock. Five minutes late, ten. Heavens, wasn't he coming? What had happened to him? I was beginning to be seriously alarmed.

But suddenly, just beside me, and then around me, and all along the pavement, a great din of shouting broke out.

It was a group of news-sellers bursting on to the streets and the Cour de Rome with the evening editions.

'Get your papers here…! *La France…! La Cocarde…! La Patrie…!*' and I don't know what else. 'New scandal on the Stock Exchange…! Read all about it…! M. Martigny arrested!'

He was in Mazas prison!! Martigny! Actually Martigny! And someone next to me said to his neighbour: 'He thought he was above it all, that one, never seemed to get his hands dirty like the rest of them, always seemed to keep a distance, just so he could plan his frauds better… what a crook!'

Some time afterwards, I received a letter from him, posted from Mazas. But I was cured of holiday retreats and I quietly left him to his.

Farewell, friend. When I think back on all these stories, I want to shake you warmly by the hand.

VII

To the Same

I opened my *Le Gaulois* this morning and out popped the name of M. Plantesol. Noël Plantesol, deputy in the National Assembly, it means nothing to you? Yet he has several excellent reports to his name, on sugar production, another on the waste disposal industry, and a third, the most significant, in support of a project to restore morality to the public streets.

I know something about it, it was I who corrected the proofs!

Which is not without its piquant element, and if Gallex the painter had been nicer to me I would have offered him a motif worthy of his modernistic approach: Josiane de Valneige collaborating in the raising of the nation's morals!

I do not tell you this, my dear, in order to diminish M. Plantesol, he performs that service very well himself; and that is exactly what I have against him, because at one time I believed in him and I would have been very happy to have believed much longer.

I made his acquaintance when I was at a table with a group of friends at Les Ambassadeurs for the preview of the Salon.

He has since explained that he always went to the vernissage because he had once intended becoming a student at the Beaux Arts.

This varnish-splashing ceremony in the Champs-Elysées is truly most strange. The only people there, all gathered on the pretext of being interested in art, are the ones who couldn't give tuppence for it! If it's genuine fun you want, laughter, youth, love, don't look there. But it is terribly smart.

Well, I was greatly surprised to meet a man there who wasn't smart at all, but better than that.

A tall dark-haired man with eyes that spoke more swiftly than his tongue. And, my dear, what a voice! It resonated like a tolling bell; and the gestures that went with it!

As for what he said? Plenty of others have said the same, and indeed he repeated his own words; but for me it was all brand new and irresistible. Incidentally, I am not at all displeased to be telling you this story, because it will oblige you to acknowledge that I am not cut from any ordinary cloth.

Oh yes, it was very strange to hear M. Plantesol in that kind of setting! He had an oratorical and patriotic constitution. Ideas about society, about reforms, about the poor, about the grandeur of politics and the country shot out of him like rockets.

Ah, those superb ideas, I was literally carried away by them; and those rolling sentences!

I'm the sort of person who, when anyone talks to me about my country, fills with emotion, and I had never heard talk like this.

So it was true, then, his type still existed? The altruist, enthusiast, firebrand, achiever? How good it must be to be close to such a man, to be loved by him and to love him!

I had had enough of spiritless little affairs and, I don't know why, I felt myself instantly at one with Plantesol in an adventure that was just beginning.

In the afternoon, I took my Plantesol on a tour of the sculptures.

The mauve dress I was wearing for the first time at this preview of fashion, my dress and he both scored a triumph. He gave no sign of being put out by it, or embarrassed. On the contrary, he seemed as proud as a peacock to be seen alongside a woman whom everyone stared at and who swapped wordless little smiles with other women as they made their way through the exhibition rooms, among the benches outside and round those lawns that look as sleek as the hair on a baby's head.

'Look! Who's Josiane de Valneige with?'

A few days later everyone knew, and they were saying: 'She's with her politician.'

Kindly believe, my dear, that if I had wanted a minister, I would have had one. It is hardly a rare species, even though totally lacking in interest and, for a woman, any decorative value.

The minister of today is indistinguishable from the minister of tomorrow, and how could it be otherwise, for the same trappings accompany each of them in turn. They live for a day against a backdrop of gold-chained ushers and they die. There are in nature, it appears, insects whose life-history is the same. And then, it can't be helped, but the frock-coated splendour of their office leaves me cold; their ladies can keep them!

With Plantesol at least I had air, I had space: nothing yet done, all to do. Would there not be happiness and fulfilment in being associated with his uplifting ideas, in lending a hand, in featuring, I too, in my own small way, in the press reports – newspapers which otherwise only recorded my presence at launch parties for a new champagne, at first nights or at Longchamp, among the lists of notable courtesans?

Yes, I was seduced by the prospect of having for my very own a great man on the rise, seduced also by his noble merits, his convictions, his detachment from all that was not directed at the general good.

Oh, how impressively he would say: 'France…! The people…! To work and suffer for the people!'

One day it moved me so much I was brought to tears, and declared my Plantesol to be unique.

It was at this period that I came to be seen so frequently in the public gallery of the Chamber of Deputies during sittings. A newspaper asked one day: 'For whose sake can it be that Josiane de Valneige attends with such devotion?'

…And indeed it was highly compromising for me.

I ended up having my own acknowledged seat in the gallery. Some of the diplomats nearby made eyes at me; others, less Parisian, did me the honour of taking me for a spy. A funny lot, the diplomatic corps!

As for me, it got to the stage where, from my elevated position, I learnt to recognise our legislators by the back of their heads. I contemplated them, all the same, with a degree of respect. It did not last, and it is impossible to imagine anything less inspiring. And we women are accused of talking without having anything to say! But the least among us talking to her tradespeople knows her business better, brings more talent to it, and even wit!

While I listened to our great patented orators, I watched my Plantesol. He was in the horseshoe-shaped body of the chamber, not sitting but standing, alert and handsome as a lion, a very learned lion, naturally. He had a lorgnette which he kept training on me, lovingly. And I thought: 'Ah, when he speaks, then we'll see what eloquence is! Among all this crowd of upstarts, we'll finally hear an apostle, one who is pure, one who is true!'

And my Plantesol assumed fantastical proportions.

'Work, my dear, work,' I used to tell him. 'Get something done, quickly.'

And I assure you, my friend, in the role of Egeria – what woman has not longed to play it? – I was really good.

I have to say that Plantesol, to do him justice, did indeed do something: he had a hand, at least, in the appointment – as postman – of a cousin of the angelic Gérard and the promotion of my god-parent Desormeau in the tax office.

Towards six o'clock, when shouting-matches and calls-to-order had succeeded each other to everyone's satisfaction, I would go and wait for him in rue de Bourgogne. I sent my carriage away, and there, outside the side door, the artists' entrance, I paced up and down like a young lover – me, Josiane de Valneige – in the presence nearby of M. Sully, a very stony statue.

At last, my Plantesol appeared… and then, my friend… then we would both walk, in the gathering dusk, to his home, to where my Plantesol lived, in a very un-Parisian district, almost unheard-of, rue Monsieur-le-Prince.

What do you say to that? The height of romance, no?

It was on the third floor of an old grey house, two rooms with books on deal shelves, portraits of M. Thiers and M. Gambetta, a plaster bust of The Republic wearing the deputy's sash, with his medal on the base; a strip of cheap carpet on the floor; pink calico curtains at the window, almost falling off their rails, a table with newspapers, printed reports, tobacco pipes and, on the back of the chair, his writing jacket; next door, in a box room, his bed, and a plank shelf, upon which stood pots of preserves and jars of goose confit sent up from the Midi, and under which he kept his clothes and the satchel he slung across his shoulders when he went out visiting his supporters.

In this cubby-hole, my Plantesol seemed all the greater to me. Yes, it was exactly where a man like him, rising above the day-to-day, ought to live. It was simple, spartan and evocative.

And I couldn't begin to tell you the pleasure it gave me to desert my comforts and luxuries from time to time, my busy life and my public face, for this out-of-the-way corner where I truly believed some unused part of my heart was going to start beating.

At first, he was more than ready to allow me that pleasure.

'Yes, let's go back,' he would say, 'since its impoverished state appeals to you. For me in fact it's a source of pride.'

For a fortnight we spent many well-filled hours there. I make no complaint about Plantesol, but our pleasures owed nothing to his prowess: who wouldn't be brilliant with me? Everything points only one way; anything different is out of the question. Yes, I don't suppose that little bed in rue Monsieur-le-Prince was ever expecting to see such fun!

But that was not what I had come all this way for. It was the visionary expression on my Plantesol's face when he spoke, as if from the benches, here in his humble home: this was love!

'Yes, speak some more,' I would say. 'Tell me everything in your soul... speak just for me... it moves me, it makes me feel good... it's what drew me to you in the first place, and it's why I feel we'll stay together.'

And, my dear, he did speak... he was as voluble as anyone could ask... but I'll tell you how easily it came to him!

Oh, Jean, my poor Jean, have you guessed...? It was always the same speech!

All the things he had told me that morning at Les Ambassadeurs he served up to me again in portions, with the same intonation, the same gestures! Not a single new idea, not a single word changed, not a comma...

He had his indignations off by heart, and there was one particular line about the progress of democracy with some especially striking image about the sweat of the people that came up with appalling regularity...!

Ah, commercial traveller, phoney, away with you!

Sometimes, getting towards the end, he would stop, a little worried, and interrupt himself: 'Was there something you didn't like...? Do you disagree...? But you see, it's the fires of inspiration, I'm making it up as I go along... improvising... it's as if I was in an arena in front of hundreds of thousands...'

The only thing he had in front of him was a woman in distress.

Was this the force that had so stirred me and set me, as I thought, on the road to love? My good qualities, such as they are, a certain enthusiasm and the desire to throw myself into things, had already carried me to lofty heights. I thought I was very close to experiencing something altogether new and now the building on the Capitol was crumbling.

In place of the people's tribune I had dreamed of, that my imagination and my heart were already celebrating, a second-rate dentist, no better than anyone else!

However, I might perhaps have forgiven him this first let-down. After all, there was some good in him, his ideas were not lies. He was trying to convince me of them through his use of words, as he might the simple-minded wife of an influential voter. But his life was still this mediocre life, which he accepted and which had seduced me, for my part, by seeming genuinely exceptional.

But one day he said to me: 'Let's go to your place, do you mind?'

By the next day his own place had become a contemptible dump! The day after that he was suggesting that he loved me even more passionately in my big Louis XIV bed, as I must no doubt have noticed...

Oh, the joker! Now he didn't want anything more to do with his rue Monsieur-le-Prince!

What Monsieur required was chocolate, served in a cup that had belonged to Marie Antoinette... he wished to read his

Drôme and Vaucluse Messenger in the mornings, propped up against my English lace pillow... and he chucked the chin of the angelic Gérard as if she were the chambermaid... and he would have liked nothing better than to know how a certain wine in my cellar was coming on, a wine that the Duc de L*** had sent me from his estate.

It was comic and saddening.

I certainly don't hold him up for blame in any of this, my Plantesol, I understand it well enough. I admit that people do not have too bad a time of it at Josiane de Valneige's house. It is the very reason why they come, and I laugh at it.

But I would have preferred my Plantesol a little less susceptible to human nature.

By what right, you will ask? Who am I to say that? By no right at all, my dear, just that I must have been a fool, a fantasist, to work up such a head of steam in his honour.

Ah, my illusion didn't last long! What I loved in my Plantesol was the very thing he turned out not to be. When I saw I was on the wrong track, that I had been stupid to expect something back in return for my expenditure of idealism and credulity, that once again I would have to give up hope of feeling the little creature astir inside me, I was very quickly cured.

That's the last time you'll catch me believing in fine gentlemen of the old school, and I tell you, it's a shame, because with my very own Plantesol, it would have been charming!

Without explaining any of my causes for disappointment, I dropped him. He was very astonished. And, promptly, he sent me some roses.

Then I applied myself to seeking my happiness elsewhere. Who knows where I shall find it, or if I shall ever find it?

****

P. S. – I am opening my letter again, dear friend, to say that politics has, however, not always been so disappointing. From a practical point of view, it's not so bad. The cousin of a minister put me in the way of a deal one day that brought in a net gain of five hundred thousand francs. With which I have the honour to bid you a fond farewell.

VIII

Jean Leblois to Josiane de Valneige

I don't want to sound flattering, my dear Josiane, or disagreeable, whichever you choose, but you fill me with amazement.

Do you know how much I depend on your letters? They are a feast, and if you had deprived me of them I would have held it against you for ever.

Your envelopes regularly get to me towards the end of the day. These little things, with their distant scent of Paris and of one Parisian in particular, bring me hours of pleasure out here.

But my selfishness is not so advanced that it leaves me indifferent to the painful reversals your heart has endured. It is marvellous and it is touching to be witness to this sort of struggle and to see a woman like you on the quest for the Golden Fleece… of happiness.

Your attempts, up to now, have not been brilliantly successful, I agree, and if I wasn't certain that a day will come when, at a stroke, you will be fully compensated, I would feel extremely sorry for you…

But I am confident, the miracle will happen just when you least expect it.

Perhaps the fault is yours, my dear; your demands are too severe, you want amazing things. Alas, they are in short supply. Life is a lot more simple than you imagine, and the true way to be happy, the surest, consists perhaps in not seeking too far.

But I can hear your answer from here: 'I am the way I am, and nothing will change me!'

Indeed; and deep down I congratulate you for being the way you are; the tiniest change would be a shame!

I expect you'll be going to the ball at the Opéra tonight. And will Josiane de Valneige make herself beautiful? Who knows, maybe the Opéra is where she will strike gold…

I daren't admit to you that the idea of a ball at the Opéra keeps buzzing in my head!

Oh, how nice it would be to run off to Paris and have a little fun!

The intrigues, the rustle of silk, bare shoulders, music that lifts the spirits, corks popping! Just thinking about it makes me itch. Lucky Parisians!

As for me, I'm off to play my game of billiards at the café du Commerce and try to win my drinks making pots and cannons off old Grenichet, the deputy mayor.

Chasing the Dream

This, my dear friend, is what makes existence beautiful!
I kiss you on your cheeks, next to that little place of olden days...

IX

Josiane de Valneige to Jean Leblois

You make me smile, my dear friend, with this ball of yours at the Opéra. So you still believe in them!

Dear me! Everyone trying to be desperately smart, and those hired Louis XIII costumes put through their paces by generations of dancers at so much per twirl!

It's not just a sorry business, it's soul-destroying.

What makes you think a woman more than usually in need of distraction would look in that direction?

Two circuits, on the arm of a gentleman whose black suit is as stiff as it is inevitable, round corridors packed with thoroughly coarse strangers; half an hour in one's box spotting through one's lorgnette club members who haven't even considered it might be a good idea to adjust their manners for the occasion; then the eternal supper, oysters and cold roast to the fore, along with the eternal ice bucket; and to cap it all, electric lighting, which is undoubtedly for Parisian women's complexions the worst invention imaginable.

It's thin stuff, admit it, and the great days are long past. What do we have now? And where does one turn for a little life and vigour?

The occasions when one might feel like being beautiful are becoming rare and to put it bluntly the busiest people in this field at present are the undertakers.

Yet... yes, there is a yet; if these yets didn't exist life really would be intolerable.

I had received, then, in my role as a pretty woman, an invitation to a party to be given one evening by the Journalists.

I don't know what you think of them; I have known and spent time with some delightful ones.

For several weeks, as it happened, I accompanied one of our most widely-read theatre critics to the premieres. He had taken a liking to me because I looked very good in one of the two dress circle seats the theatres gave him. He never asked anything of me, what's more, except to allow it to be thought that he might well be asking something more!

The evenings with him were really very interesting. It was all a question of who might come over to say hello, pay court to him as he sat there, applaud or jeer with him. The actors on stage always had half an eye on him, and, when my friend was kind enough to guffaw with laughter, a success was assured.

I also received my share of homage, of flattery; and the most prominent people would lean across and want to know my opinion, as if I knew all about the theatre. The poor devils imagined I would have some influence over the review!

What power these journalists have! It would make you quake in your boots if you weren't on their side.

Personally, I always make kind remarks about their cleverness, and they return the compliment!

This one, for example, mentions my name with rare punctiliousness in the gossip pages of his major broadsheet; that other one builds me a reputation as a talented sportswoman, which does no harm to one's reputation, even in matters of love!

Little Dumontel, especially, favours me with his good offices: in his columns I am everywhere, in different places at the same time: in Monte Carlo and at a first night at the Bouffes, in Trouville and on the Terrace of Saint-Germain! Yesterday I went to a house-warming party at someone's smart little mansion; today I have disappeared to some jealously guarded love nest out in the sticks. It's extremely flattering, and it at least gives me the illusion that my existence might be of interest to someone.

There is another journalist who, for his part, never misses an opportunity to be disagreeable: because one day I refused – oh, flatly! – to be his guest of honour at a decadent dinner party. I console myself with the thought that if I had gone it would have turned out exactly the same.

But I did go to this special Journalists' party. It was being given, apparently, for a good cause, for every journalist these days is a little charity worker.

There is nothing more boring than getting dressed at eleven at night and telling oneself: in an hour from now I shall be having fun!

As a general rule, it is always a waste of effort.

Well, that evening, the rule proved untrue.

The concert before the party came to an end, and all the stars, when their own theatres emptied, had come over to join us.

What was charming about it was the feeling of being together in one big family, those who bask in their reputations mingling with those who make them.

Josiane de Valneige, in these surroundings, nevertheless made her own little impression. Take my word for it!

While the dance floor was being set up, the swarm of familiar worshippers, people eager to impress, fell on me. Fat Taddéma, Baron Taddéma, if you please, the same man who had informed me that he would unhesitatingly bestow on me his Venezuelan barony, along with his hand, in exchange for a little comfort – he had lost all his money in the fleshpots – the baron himself came over to deploy his charms.

But I had had enough of all these old acquaintances. Since this was new territory to me, might not chance send me a semblance of novelty?

Who knows, among all these artists, these writers, these Parisians of a particular type, perhaps there would be one with enough about him to attract me, to cast over me his not too well-used charm, and allow me to cast on him a not too sour eye.

They say that journalists today have willingly become good family men, steady types always home in time for dinner. But it really would be a shame if they were all of the same stamp and if there wasn't amongst their number at least one left: one funny, enterprising, cheeky little fellow, with sufficient understanding to appreciate when a woman is bored and come to her rescue.

'Madame de Valneige, may I escort you to the buffet?'

'Valneige, you won't refuse me this waltz?'

'Josiane, a rose for your corsage?'

In those three steps, and their differently modulated tones, I became acquainted with little Carbonnel from the *Moniteur des Boulevards*, dark-haired, monocle in his eye, dressed to the nines, and with an impertinent little look that suited him perfectly.

I don't quite know how he did it, but that little man had my attention immediately, set my head spinning with his newspaper chatter, his gaiety, his energy and also… no, I daren't admit it, his attractively triumphant manner.

From time to time, when he pushed his way through the dancers with me, some of the women threw him admiring glances from under their eye-masks; others caught his hand as he passed, held on to it for a second, and they were not just people out of the crowd but women of standing. And as for him…!

'You see,' he said, 'I'm not too badly thought of here…! I'm fit to be seen in public… you do know, Josiane, it's you alone I want to love… love the way I know how, with excitement, with tact, with a bit of devilry… do you think a writer making love is the same as a grocer making love…? But you, my dear, what do you know about it? You've only ever known rich people's way of loving, and so-called smart people's… you should try the other way, the only real way, the only one that doesn't go grey as it gets older!'

He filled my ears with these follies, little snippets, again and again, during our endless strolls round the ballroom.

Sometimes he would suddenly whisk me on to the floor to join a quadrille; or at others he would pin me in a corner with his jokes, his remarks on the people passing before us, his funny stories, witticisms and gestures which had a gallantry and a boldness I found very seductive.

'Love me, I want you to love me, you do love me! And the nicest part is that it will be for myself, isn't that right, Josiane? I have nothing to offer you but a bit of flattery in my paper... what now? So that's just a joke to you, I suppose?'

Quite right, it was an absolute joke to me! But Roger Carbonnel was not.

You know, dear friend, I've always been an avid reader. So you'll understand why I'm fond of this particular chapter in my story, the episode with a little journalist, which brings to mind similar characters in Balzac's books.

Little Carbonnel didn't actually put his name to many articles, but he told me there were plenty of journalists to whom that applied. What does he do, then? He exercises his wit, he is indiscreet, naughty, just a little bit – and enjoyably – bitchy, and just to hear him talk is to find him adorable. He entertained me, on his own account, better than a dozen gossip columns together, and I laughed as I hadn't laughed for a long time. So much so that at one point he said: 'This won't do...! I hope you don't imagine I'm here just to amuse Madame...? I'm worth better than that...'

I had wounded his self-esteem, and his vexed little look was a treat. Never mind, never mind, little Carbonnel, no one is taking you for a mere entertainer, a peddler of witticisms...

don't look so cross… here, this is for you…

And as we happened to be standing by the buffet just then – as we frequently were! – I gave him my glass and I emptied his.

It was silly, romantic, a hoary old gesture, but I felt like it and it gave him pleasure.

At supper he had reserved one of the small tables and managed things so that we enjoyed a space of our own in the middle of the crowds.

We had had many dances together; he had made me enjoy dancing, which, honestly, I didn't think was my forte. What pleasure then to feel young and energetic, to close your eyes and let yourself go, just go and keep on going as long as you can. But now, sitting down, a pleasant tiredness came over me, a well-being that pervaded every part of me.

He sat very close to me, then, with his chair, edged even closer. All around us there was laughter, songs, the headiness of revelry late into a beautiful night.

And putting a hand on mine, looking at me, or rather drinking me with his eyes, with his other hand, on the table cloth, little Carbonnel wrote me verses in pencil and read them out.

I don't remember how the lines went exactly, but I can confirm, my dear friend, that they were very neatly turned.

When the music, from way off, in the ballroom, started up again, everything in my head seemed to sing, to swing, to crackle with fire.

Do you know, your Josiane was, if not plastered as you horrible men like to say, then at least gently tipsy, the only time in her life! Ah, it is nice, it's delicious, to feel that little fizzing in your brain, and hurrah for the wine of Champagne which lends a rosy glow to all you see and feel! Ah, and he was good at keeping the glasses filled, was little Carbonnel; and what an enjoyable surprise to feel this tipsiness spreading through me, spreading to my every part!

I stood up, laughter on my lips and in my eyes, an immense and motiveless joy in my heart, needing to see still more light, hear still more merriment.

But suddenly, at one of the ballroom doors, I spotted little Carbonnel. Next to him, a commissionaire in braid and chains from the Hôtel Continental, where we were, was holding an overcoat over one arm, my long otter coat over the other...

And little Carbonnel was signalling me to come over.

Ah, these journalists! They can make you do anything they want, and they know exactly what that is...!

And when I was at his side, he said, speaking slowly and clearly – and in a manner, my word, that brooked no dissent: 'And now, let us go home!'

What did I do? You know already, my friend.

I slipped into my fur, I put on my hat, I straightened my gloves as best I could... and we left.

Ah, such a marvellous evening... and if you will permit me, such a marvellous night!

But alas, it could be marvellous only if there was no aftermath: one of life's windfalls, and not life itself. My happiness with the little journalist from the party was and could only be, like a newspaper article, a thing of a single day.

That was how I took it, and perhaps that is why I still think of it with a smile.

X

To the Same

I come now, my dear friend, to the Fleurignac chapter. Yes, you read that correctly: Fleurignac.

'What, him too?'

'Him too, yes. And more so than any of the others.'

Many women, from the Duchess of B*** to that poor Etiennette, the dancer from the Folies Modernes, have loved Fleurignac, handsome Fleurignac of the Théâtre Parisien, but none with anything like the intensity or devotion that I might have displayed.

How could anyone watch, listen to this great actor and not love him?

His looks are exactly right: a head of dark hair, a face

74

of unexpected pallor and features deeply incised by both the passions he has acted out and the ones he has felt. There is no one in Paris of more striking appearance.

And certainly, in shop-keepers' windows, his photograph always produces a terrific effect.

Fleurignac, old chum, is from Marseilles, which means I don't need to tell you how passionate he can be and how vigorously he throws himself into every least thing; nor to say that his physical presence is magnetic enough to stir the hardest of spectators' hearts.

Imagine the effect, then, on a mere woman!

I loved him. And to think when I first saw him on stage I thought he was awful, and even ridiculous!

But charm works in its own mysterious way, and one morning you wake up head over heels in love and desperate to have the man to yourself.

I wrote to him, without stopping to think he must be immune to fan letters. He admitted that he received at least two such letters a day on average and if he didn't get any he considered his day a failure…!

But my letter caught his eye, it seems, and he sent me back a few lines that went straight to my heart.

For a fortnight, Fleurignac and I – who were both completely free – allowed ourselves the luxury of playing out a courtship, preserving the bounds of polite formality, spinning the threads of the perfect platonic love affair.

And I can assure you that this was by no means the least rewarding part of our story.

We appeared in public together, and before we had actually done anything we were already being talked of as a couple.

Finally I became his mistress, and for the first time I instantly felt that terrible and yet delicious thing – because it really lets you know you are alive – called jealousy.

Fleurignac was mine, but it did not prevent him from murmuring words of love every evening to other women, from folding them in his arms – and what arms!

It did no good telling myself it's absurd, it's his job, it's 'only pretend', I still underwent torments, often strong enough to bring me to tears.

And when I stupidly confessed to this weakness, he shrugged his shoulders, smiled a masterful smile and said: 'Come along to the theatre then, come to my dressing room and you'll see!'

I went along constantly.

I was present while he made up, and for his costume changes.

Oh, that little room! Its walls were filled with oriental hangings, photographs of Fleurignac in his principal roles, photographs of his fellow actors with glowing dedications, reproductions of sets, cuttings from newspapers.

It made for such an alluring atmosphere, full of light and human warmth, I found it quite intoxicating.

And I shall always have before my eyes the image of Fleurignac standing there in front of his mirror, arms bare, vividly outlined, doing his face and all the time chattering away, whilst I sat there, in his atmosphere, close to him, in a low armchair, looking lovingly at him, breathing him in.

Yes, the dresser, the call-boy, various friends would come in and interrupt us; and sometimes the dressing room door would swing ajar and give a glimpse in profile of a passing female figure, powdered, cheeks and lips rouged, eyes outlined with kohl, a soubrette or coquette; but most of the time we were just there, as if at home, the two of us together.

And yes, that's really how it was: we were left to ourselves; and I think on purpose, because it was known that a kind of honeymoon was taking place up in that room.

Nothing was more charming than enjoying such intimacy a mere step away from an auditorium packed with All Paris.

Good old All Paris, which we were part of ourselves: if it had suspected how completely, during the intervals, it was forgotten up in that little room!

As soon as he had left the stage, Fleurignac would meet me there. I would welcome him with my heart on fire and still trembling from his impassioned performance. And he would repeat for me the words he had been saying to the heroine of the play, adapting them to our own situation, with subtle variations that were so delicately telling.

And then… and then, yes… there were kisses and kisses again!

'My dearest Josiane, she is everything I love,' he would say to anyone who would listen.

And to me he never tired of saying that his whole life henceforward would flow like a river channelled between the twin banks of his art and his love.

At one point, the rumour on the boulevards even had it that I was going to marry Fleurignac.

Marry him, why not? You know that the excellent M. Aubertin had sought and obtained a divorce. But I have never been attracted to that idea and I denied it forcefully. Become Mme Fleurignac! And what then? Happiness does not depend on these formalities, and what counts for me, the thing I'm looking for, is happiness for its own sake.

But if I had no thought of marrying my Fleurignac – although marriage is quite the fashion just now in our less respectable half of society – I did have another idea.

Picture this, my friend: your Josiane de Valneige, for a while, really thought she would go in for the theatre!

Yes, I had developed a real passion! It seemed to me that nothing in the world would be better or more splendid!

How good it must feel to bask in the audience's applause, and for a woman, how triumphant, how intoxicating! A life of excitement, of legitimate fame built on successes that everyone can acclaim, what a change from the other life.

You are no longer Josiane de Valneige, you are an artist; you do something that raises you in the public eye, without losing any of your qualities in the process, or any of your prestige as a woman of beauty – quite the reverse! I would have seen my profile posted up on huge hoardings in beautiful colours, shimmering like some fine fabrics. And I would have given interviews to journalists.

But there was more to this belief in my vocation, to speak without embarrassment, than such fantasies as those. My dear, laugh if you like, I now believed in art, in the existence of a whole heap of things beyond the comprehension of bourgeois people, things far above our current petty concerns.

That was sweet of me, don't you think? But it came quite naturally: Fleurignac and his powerful enthusiasms, his ways of seeing and feeling, were rubbing off on me. I was Fleurignac's disciple.

'Oh, teach me!' I said to him.

'What?'

'What you know!'

'You don't ask much, do you?'

'I want to have talent too... I will have if you help... it must be such fun!'

And I recited scenes taken from the plays he was in; I also tried some cabaret songs out on him, in the style of Judic or Yvette Guilbert, because I hadn't yet settled on what sort of talent I'd have. One day I even performed many a dainty curtsey and step in the manner of Loïe Fuller, in my pink silk dressing gown.

I didn't make anything of any of this, but I am persuaded, my dear friend, that I would have enjoyed as much success as any other woman!

A look would have been enough, a kind word or, to put it in a nutshell, some love from Fleurignac.

Ah, what worlds of possibility I had built on that love! Women are like that: we invest all our capital in one person; when it fails, everything collapses. After so many setbacks with so many different types of men, Fleurignac was for me the lover, the friend, the heart, the flesh, the pride, the giving of one's entire self, so to speak, and I had said to myself: 'At last!'

One evening, I told him the story of my life, the long series of defeats I had suffered, the lost illusions, and I described the state I was in when he met me. His response was magnificent: 'Yes, you have been waiting... you have been searching for a long time... but it was all in order to find one man: me. We were made for each other, made never to be parted...! Forget – I, yes, I shall make you forget – those times of doubt and discouragement and solitude... I am here!'

That was true bliss, or at least as close as I had ever come to it.

To show you how genuinely I believed this was the definitive happiness, we lived for ourselves alone, for no one but us: I never saw anyone else but him, I had shut my door to the world with a joy I was positively proud of; and he, for his part, never left my side except to attend rehearsals and on the evenings when he was working.

During that time, the dishes served at Josiane de Valneige's were homely stews, because he was very fond of them and I found the idea very simple and intimate. It made the house smell of lives shared, of lovers.

We had also agreed that he would move out of his little bachelor flat in rue Daunou. What did he need a place of his own for, which only served as a constant reminder to me of his past, his adventures, his love affairs? There was a certain little blue sitting room which had apparently been the scene of some very extraordinary ones and whose existence I found most trying.

We would live resolutely together and everything would be shared in common.

I remember how well we did share everything in common because one evening when he had allowed himself to be dragged away to his club I was happy enough, yes, very happy, to help extricate him from an awkward situation.

I mention this, my dear friend, not to put Fleurignac down in any way. My view on these things is that a woman who claims to love a man has a duty to do anything necessary and in any circumstances for the man she loves. I mention it rather to give you a true idea of our relationship and how things worked between us.

So I had come to trust Fleurignac. Despite the sort of jolt it gave me every time I saw him on stage take a woman in his arms or press his lips to hers, in real life I was sure of him. When could he have betrayed me, and above all why? For him I was the perfect mistress, I declare it openly, and not to my own credit, for I took pleasure in being so.

That, for me, is what duty means!

To be sure of a man! Ah, my dear, there's a stupid remark you won't hear me make again! I would gladly laugh at my naivety, my blindness, if I hadn't suffered real grief because of it.

Fleurignac and most of the actors from his theatre used to take their productions on tour. Often you see sweethearts, and others, accompanying their loved ones on these tours. There are people known as camp followers, who travel round from hotel to hotel and who are pointed out to each other with secret envy by the locals.

Why wouldn't I have switched roles to become one of them and follow my Fleurignac? It would be simply charming, a little elopement, enjoying praise and laurels out in the provinces, and love on the road!

I told him nothing of my plan. But when he took me in his arms to say goodbye, I showed him my trunk and my travelling costume.

I was expecting an explosion of joy: oh, you should have seen Fleurignac's expression! No, he wasn't pleased at all, I was making him look ridiculous, it wasn't done! Then a sudden change of mood, and in the end a warm smile. We set off for Rouen.

One of Fleurignac's pleasures, dear friend, is talking about actors from the past and the difficult conditions they lived under. For the whole journey, while we were in a reserved compartment, waited on by attentive staff, treated like royalty, Fleurignac never stopped talking about a book he remembered on the subject, called *Le Roman Comique*, and it gave him visible satisfaction to assert: 'How times have changed!'

I pity those actors of the olden days! We, in contrast, found local dignitaries waiting to greet us at the station, and an apartment had been taken for us at the Hôtel de Londres on the embankment, and when we got there a reception committee of journalists was lined up either side of the entrance.

One of them even wanted to describe my hat, which I let him do with pleasure, it's the least I owe my milliner!

Fleurignac's performance was hailed as a triumph. I remember the emotions of the two of us, mine especially, which made me understand how much he meant to me.

When we arrived back at the hotel, I was the one carrying the crown of oak leaves he had been awarded, with its pretty inscription picked out in silver.

And it's a curious thing, I didn't feel the least bit awkward, walking in with this thing looped on my arm; the feeling was rather that the two of us represented a single entity.

The next morning, he wrote a number of telegrams for friends he had in the Paris press.

He meant the capital to know all about it.

And I can still see him in his shirtsleeves, hesitating between 'admirable' and 'sublime'. And in fact I was the one who told him: 'Put both! It's not worth getting into a state about things like that.'

It was just turned ten. I had a few errands to run across town. I enjoyed it, trotting round, strolling about by myself while he was resting, and I took the telegrams, leaving him ready to go back to bed, as he likes to do, windows open on to the river, which was bathed in sunlight and sending up a delicious breath of spring.

Normally, it rains in Rouen, Rouen rain is as famous as Rouen duckling: so I remember the sun that day as an exception, and also because the few hours it shone were in contrast a very sad few hours for me.

It was a little after twelve when I returned, light of step, with an excellent appetite and a contented heart.

There are days like that, when you are very happy without quite knowing why, and it is always on those days that something bad happens.

I climb the stairs, I am outside the door, I hear voices and laughter.

What's this? Who can be with Fleurignac? It's a woman, yes, a woman's voice.

A colleague from the theatre dropping in, no doubt. No, theatre women have a tone and accent all their own, you can pick an actress out in any crowd.

And the voice I could hear through the door was… oh, my friend, if you'd heard it…! It was slow, sing-song, it was heavy, horribly common, it was a village voice, a fat Normandy wife chattering under the apple trees.

That voice made an unforgettable impression on me!

What were they saying? I listened. Suddenly there was nothing but murmurs. Then, again, a laugh, several laughs.

83

So, my dear… I did the wrong thing – but every woman would have done the wrong thing – I opened the door.

The loose kind of blouse she was wearing was unbuttoned, her skirt was pulled up, revealing enormous calves that were putting ladders in her blue stockings: a girl sitting on the bed…

It was plain she had just been lying on the pillow, my pillow, because it had been smoothed out before and now there was a new hollow in it. What's more, I looked at Fleurignac and from the expression on his face, I understood everything!

Oh, my dear Jean, it was so repellent! He had just this very minute been deceiving me, here in our bedroom, with the chambermaid.

You will tell me, my friend, that a woman like Josiane de Valneige must expect everything, that she has no right to judge the behaviour of others or to be offended.

Whatever you like, perhaps you're right. But nevertheless the truth of the matter is that, just like some bourgeois housewife, or a duchess of unblemished virtue, the vomit rose in my throat.

Poor girl! Good God, no, it isn't her I'm angry at. But to think of him, though – him! – with that chambermaid, a piece of nothing! And in that very instant, the man standing there, the person who had done this to me, toppled from his lofty place in my heart, dropped completely out of it.

It was like a guillotine falling, my dear: something I couldn't do anything about, a thing that happened inside me, as if in spite of myself.

Him! Fleurignac! The only man, according to the authors he introduced me to, with a heart big enough to understand their work! My Fleurignac, the man of grand passions, love, art! Yes, it came down to this. What a collapse!

Pitifully, he tried to explain it away.

At one point, he even passed it off as a joke.

As for me, my dear, stupid to confess, I sobbed my heart out.

But it wasn't only my Fleurignac I wept for. It was everything I was losing in thus losing my love for him. If all Fleurignac's tenderness only led to this, and if it was through things like this that I was supposed to view the artistry that had so seduced me, it was over: no, no, a hundred times no!

True enough, another man – any other man – would have been free to behave the way Fleurignac did. The men I've felt nothing for, the ones whose functions were mainly to be useful and only secondarily a source of pleasure, they are and remain perfectly independent as far as I am concerned. But it is not the same when I have believed, when I have dreamed of loving someone, and when I have given some of myself.

So, my Jean, I remained a woman of ice, mute before the entreaties and the admirable scenes he acted out. He said the most amazing things, he found new heights of eloquence, none of which could overcome my pride or repair my wounded heart.

In my inner being, it was broken.

And that evening, dear friend, the Paris express received me on board again, this time alone.

I settled in my corner. A regional paper that I had unthinkingly bought was talking about Fleurignac's performance. For a long minute I stared at this sheet, thoughts in a whirl, then I screwed it into a ball and threw it out of the window…

And with every turn of the wheel carrying me forward I

seemed to feel the ditch of the past being dug ever deeper.

When I arrived home, I found my maid asleep in her bed. Ah, what an honest girl!

XI

Jean Leblois to Josiane de Valneige

Well, no, my dearest of friends, I won't say you were wrong!

And if you want to know what I really feel, that's the way I prefer you.

If you are suffering, if you are close to despair, console yourself with the thought that there are not many of you in town who suffer for such causes and who think the same way as you.

It is what distinguishes you from the Louise Martins and the Suzanne de Colognes.

I am sure that if they felt the urge to relate their own stories, there would be no place for details like yours – although, if people looked properly, they would find that inside every woman is a little secret which, if it was known, would show that she was worth a great deal more than those people might suppose.

What is this? Is your friend from the Touraine turning sanctimonious? He sounds like just the sort of man who'd know that celebrated line about fallen women.

Don't be cross with him, and don't laugh at him: it may be the very reason why you trust him.

But seriously, Josiane, is it going to go on like this?

Will you never write me a letter to say you are happy, totally happy? That you have once and for all found love, and happiness in love?

It would be so right for you! And I may add that if there is any justice, you are owed it.

With all my heart I wish you a dazzling comeback. Do not let yourself, while waiting, be overwhelmed by sadness and discouragement. Let's bury Fleurignac deep in the ground and make space for the new. I don't like to think of the beautiful Josiane being melancholy, and I hope it will not be so.

Whatever else, you can always count on my old friendship.

It cannot claim to replace everything, it is not so foolish as that. But it can serve a purpose: draw on it at any time. We'll be in touch soon, then, yes?

I take your little hands in mine and press them warmly.

P.S. Allow me, my friend, to present you with an opportunity for a little distraction amid all the dark swirls that such memories must cast round you.

You would be acting as the most delightful of friends if you were to slip down to the Louvre and take the trouble to have them send here a dozen pairs of gloves, tan, size 7 ¾, for riding.

XII

Josiane de Valneige to Jean Leblois

Alas, my friend, you were a very poor prophet when you hoped 'it would not be so'. My adventure with Fleurignac made a lasting impression.

I emerged from it entirely stripped of any faith in the future, in myself, in love, in anything at all. Very well, if that was the case, why keep trying? Since it has been proved that I am not made for happiness, or that happiness does not exist, it would be mere folly. Let's do the same as everyone else, then: forward march, eyes closed!

What's the point in hankering after midday at two in the afternoon? It's a fool's game, so three cheers for those who take life as it comes!

But that is just making arguments for the sake of it.

However much I wanted to act on them, convince myself, stifle my thoughts, this latest experience lay deep in my bones and provoked as much revolt as genuine affliction.

I remained crushed by this blow for months. What was the matter with Josiane de Valneige? People were taking notice, I can tell you!

Some asserted that my boredom, my disgust were the result of having enjoyed life too greedily – imbeciles! Others swore I had turned to morphine, to ether, a host of poisons currently much in favour and utterly wonderful, apparently.

Just between the two of us, I did think about it. But morphine, whose delights I'd heard so much about, was just another fanciful joke.

Blisters, itching under the skin, that's all. It seems I'm not cut out for that either. It's annoying!

One day a friend of mine sent me her doctor, Doctor Tardenot.

Tardenot is very well known, he specialises in our fin de siècle ailments. The best way he could think of to cure me of what he called, by a horrible name incidentally: neurasthenia – yes, imagine that, I was a neurasthenic! – was for me to take him as my lover.

Ah, wasn't that handy for him, the excellent Tardenot.

No! No more lovers! Peace: peace in the company of steady friends who would ask little of me and of whom I would not ask more than they could give.

But what a strange destiny! To be ready for love, to live only for love, to have demeaned myself in its pursuit, and never to find it! My dear, you are my witness: have I, yes or no, done everything I could to encounter it, to hold on to it? And you, after all, know more about me on that score than anyone!

But the whole business had been a torture, I had become the Tantalus of the human heart!

The moment I thought I had it in my grasp, bliss escaped me.

Sometimes everything suddenly went cold in me, at other times it was the other party who cast me back into the void, through letting me down or through turning out to be an inferior person.

Some women manage to be happy, so what is their trick? They don't have a heart, that's what. All the easier for them… perhaps it's better not to have one…

No, don't believe that, I'm lying. I'm not giving up on mine, for all the pain it has brought me. And I'm proud to be the way I am.

Be that as it may, I was apparently in the most lamentable state.

They tried to bring about a reconciliation between me and Fleurignac: if he had been some ordinary sort of lover, I would have forgiven him; but I had invested too much in him and I couldn't.

So then it was a question of who would look after me. It's a funny thing how keen people are to sympathise with a woman's troubles if those troubles happen to provide a boost for their own self-esteem!

'Come to the country with us, my dear friend! We shall console you.'

'Oh, you must come to us… you know there's always a room for you. We'll have such fun, boredom just isn't possible in my house…! Silly goose!'

I put a swift end to that kind of thing, and one morning I simply left, on my own account, without telling a soul.

I didn't need to lift a finger: the angelic Gérard organised everything, and all I had to do was come, bringing with me a weariness of Paris, of human beings and of material things.

Ah, this time, when I saw a railway station again, it was wonderful, and I leapt into the train as if I was fleeing from hell.

What happened out in the countryside? Friend, you will soon discover. But it won't all fit in one letter, or even several.

I know that just from reading the brief accounts I have put before you, haphazard and unconnected, you do not envy me my fate. How will it be when you know the rest of what I have to tell you, the most important part of all, the part that is both the most marvellous and most painful of my entire life?

The day you came to visit me and when I promised to write you regular letters, you found me in very low spirits, do you remember, my dear Jean, and in a frame of mind rare for one of those women whose paths are reputed to be strewn with roses. I was still reeling from a terrible emotional shock, and haunted by the grief and troubles of the story that had just come to an end.

Today, in order to keep my promise, it is necessary to plunge back into it!

So be it; perhaps the exercise will do me good; perhaps, underlying so many hard moments that I must revisit, there may be for me some small sweetness to rediscover.

I am going to tell the story from the very beginning, as it unfolded day by day, hour by hour, as if I was back in that time. My memory has retained every last detail; and besides, I have only to turn to the journal I kept at the time for comfort, to record my impressions as they swung between elation and misery, moment by moment.

I tremble, and yet I am already a little happier just to be taking these fading pages and living through it all again with you.

You will see whether your Josiane is blessed by fortune, whether she is wrong when she swears that all is myth and chimera; and whether it wouldn't have been entirely forgivable if she had been a hundred times worse than she is!

XIII

To the Same

Here I am, surrounded by fields, communing with... me. I'm sure you catch my drift: with myself alone. The angelic Gérard, my little dog and my pet monkey and that's it, yes that's all there is.

A surfeit of other people, a need for solitude, whatever you like to call it. It sounds so unlikely when we're talking about Josiane de Valneige, but that's how it is. We all have our own little peccadillos. Mine is to be always in search of the thing I haven't yet found, as you well know... in love with love, that poor Josiane.

Rue de Prony, with its constant luxury, its shallow infatuations that don't engage the heart, and its repeated disappointments made me dream, as I mentioned in a letter, of a little retreat in the woods. I found it at Brunoy.

Do you know of Brunoy? A little green oasis an hour from Paris, quite far enough, I promise you, to keep me from returning too often.

The house? A good, honest place, peacefully set among green lawns and a garden as white as a giant bridal bouquet.

Inside? Comfortable, good atmosphere, lifted especially by my indispensable bits and pieces which add artistic and feminine notes to offset all this bourgeois mahogany and red velvet. For example, my washstand is wholly me! Could I live without my Sèvres basins, my gold and ivory brushes, my bottles and my mirrors?

This sanctuary for self-pampering has a wide window looking on to the countryside, and in the mornings – bless me, as soon as the sun rises – I'm a changed woman, as you see – I have been leaning on the window sill in the cool of the morning and – shall I admit it? – I have been enjoying myself very much.

Watching the neighbourhood wake up, gates opening, and windows, blinds being raised, gardeners coming and going, milkmen, I don't know what: all this was absolutely new to me. Among others here, just next to me, surrounded by vast meadows full of superb cows grazing in bovine content, is a magisterial manor house, home to the inflated pride of a prince of the Parisian goldsmith's trade and sponsor, naturally, of the new church bell.

A little further off, scattered in a sea of greenery, are smiling gardens and pretty villas which disgorge, from eight in the morning, making for the Paris train like an army of flustered crows, office workers, bankers, ministry clerks who then, from nightfall to morning, return to forget their desk-bound lives amid the freshness of the fields. And amongst all the good Parisians, who would feel lost if they couldn't come and enjoy some country air in the summer, there are some very amusing types, and I am inventing little background stories for each of them. Dealers in household goods who have forgotten where they started from – doubtless lighting the gas lamps for their bosses – and have adopted the manners of club-men, waddle along with their soft grey hats tipped over one ear. Great ladies... of the grocery world, on the arm of their paunchy and beribboned husbands, coming here to consume the profits from their sugar and their coffee. It makes you squirm with laughter, my dear!

There are, I must say, some handsome carriages to be seen as well, passing up and down the roads of this peaceful spot. But not as smart as mine, which means I shall still make my effect, alas, and I shall still be a topic of gossip.

None of this is very thrilling, as you can tell, and I'm sure the only distraction from my boredom will be taking walks. But perhaps I shall thereby escape the grief that undermines me and at the same time weighs me down; and then I do so need to forget the Plantesols, the Fleurignacs and Co., all the puppets, all the dummies at whose side I have never found what my heart is mad enough to insist on looking for!

XIV

To the Same

Sick at heart, weary, seized by both a sense that she has had enough of herself and the need to start living again, eager for powerful emotions and sensations, for refined pleasures, for love's sweet fragrance, see how Josiane now yields to the indefinable charms of nature.

It seems to me that the breath of the new season is refreshing my thirsting heart; it seems to me that in every smiling flower a promise is hidden, that the murmuring stream and the whispering trees are transmitting messages of love, and that this renewal of nature is forcing a rejuvenated sap through my scorched veins.

I am a woman who has run the gamut, done it all, yet I

feel within me these virgin-like aspirations, this longing for innocence, this thirst for pure air. I day-dream like a young girl, and as I swim in this exciting sea of ideals my old desires sink and drown, my ineffectual and unhealthy infatuations, my past and my tawdry fame.

To love!!! To love! Oh, yes, the problem that never goes away! To see my weary heart mirrored in the limpid gaze of another! To tremble with unfeigned happiness in the embrace of another! To let fall on my cheeks a tear that is real! To have my emotions shudder, for once, with the same pleasure my body knows, and to feel that I have not just lent my flesh but given my heart.

Forgive me, dear friend… but did you not encourage me to write to you without artifice and to say anything?

I am going to tell you therefore that one day, walking with no particular purpose along one of the many shady footpaths, I ran into a couple, a man and a woman, who looked very interesting.

A mother and son, probably, and both of them in full mourning. The widow – I say widow because I noticed the white band round her black crepe hat – was a distinguished-looking woman and still very beautiful in spite of her rather tired features. She was looking up at this son with much tenderness and pride while he spoke to her in an adorably confiding manner. Two exceptional people!

He was handsome, in an unusual way. Well now, I'd like to picture him for you, since you must already be intrigued.

Tall, slender, with something sad about the way he carries himself. There is something delicate, too, about his pale face, and whatever passions may be contained in his large, soft eyes are hinted at only by their dark gleam. With his thick, slightly wavy hair framing a twenty-year-old's unlined forehead, his whole aura is indefinably alluring. Can I put it this way, he resembles a Florentine poet from the great days of Lorenzo de' Medici, as portrayed in a statuette I have at home? Perhaps, and if you are willing, that's what we shall call him.

As you might imagine, they made a distinct impression on me, and I stood watching them until they were out of sight. Who were they? I would dearly have liked to know.

Another encounter, which I found less charming, was with that fat Baron de Raincourt!

Fortunately, I only saw him from behind, and that awful hair-style of his with its exaggerated parting running right down to the nape of his neck. If I hadn't spotted that, and if he had turned and seen me, goodbye to peace and quiet!

So to avoid him I went back home in something of a rush.

'Goodness!' the angelic Gérard exclaimed. 'You look all of a tizzy, madame. What's happened?'

'Happened…? What's happened is that imbecile Baron de Raincourt has taken it into his head to come to Brunoy and he's disturbing my peace. The old fool completely ruined my walk, because I have to say, since I tell you everything, dear Gérard, that I was miles away at the time. Before that old woodenhead came along, I'd just seen an amazingly beautiful young man. Try to find out for me who he is. He's tall, he's youthful, he had his mother on his arm, she was wearing mourning, the pair of them were out walking, in the direction of the forest. I don't know any more than that. See what you can find out…'

Two days later, for Gérard is a good spy, she came in triumphantly with her report when she brought me my morning chocolate. Without appearing to have any such intention, she had managed to extract from the gardener from next door everything he knew on the subject.

'They're unassuming people who live very simply. Mme Duvert is the widow of a departmental head in the ministry of defence who died of a chest complaint a year ago and left her with only a modest pension. Her son, Paul Duvert, whom she adores, is a perfect young man, capable of great achievements, as he was a brilliant student, but because of his delicate health a little too much tied to his mother's apron strings. They live in a little house on the edge of Sénart forest, where they retired to after the father's death.'

And that's it, I don't know any more than that. But what I do know is that I am still under the spell cast by that youthful and poetic vision. Am I destined not to be quite as tranquil as all that in this supposed retreat of mine?

The weather was delicious. I spent hours going for walks or carriage rides, I was out of doors all the time.

A few days afterwards, I set off in the direction of Sénart forest. This forest interested me.

I was striding boldly along – you wouldn't have recognised me – oblivious of my carriage, left on the main Epinay road, and of the storm that was rumbling in the background, when suddenly I realised I had ventured too far and lost my way. Already, fat drops of rain were beginning to fall on my dress of pink lawn, wetting my open-work stockings and the little shoes that were more accustomed to plush cushions.

So, startled like a bird caught out of its nest, I hurried ahead, looking along each path, throwing questioning glances at the sky and the ground, when suddenly I saw, emerging from the trees close by, a young lad also in a hurry.

'I say, my friend,' I called, going over to him, 'can you show me the path that goes to les Alouettes?' I remembered leaving my carriage not far from there.

'Ain't from these parts. Don't know the place,' he said with a gormless air. 'But, hey, just up there, at the keeper's house, they'll tell you all right.'

A few metres further on, a roof of red tiles stood out sharply against the grey sky.

That's it then, I thought. Come on, chin up!

And hitching up my skirts like a true countrywoman, I made for the house as directed. There I would wait for the storm to end whilst these good people hurried off to fetch my carriage.

But suddenly there was a tremendous clap of thunder and, frightened out of my wits, I almost fell into the arms of the forest warden coming to see who it was stumbling up to his door.

'The young man's not hurt, he isn't hurt, calm yourself, pretty lady!'

Totally bewildered, I understood not a word the good fellow was saying.

'Just a moment,' I gasped, 'I don't know what you mean… I've come to ask for shelter until this storm blows itself out and I can get back to my carriage up on the road.'

The forest keeper realised I knew nothing, and hastened to explain, in obsequious tones: 'Then come in, madame, but I've got to warn you straight off, surprises like this don't do anyone no good. We've got a poor young feller through there who's still out cold. Brigitte's rubbing his temples for all she's worth and he's still not come round. When the storm broke I was just finishing my rounds and I heard this bicycle bell ringing behind me, all urgent, and this bicycle hurtled past like a thunderbolt. Then crash! I see this young man that's riding it hit a marker stone a few metres further up the path. I run as fast as my old legs will let me and, lordy, he's in a terrible state. I pick him up, I get my arm round him and, as it's not so far from here, we manage to drag ourselves back to the cottage. But, bless me, the effort's been too much and he's passed out!'

'Let's go and see him,' I replied, 'and if I can be of any use…'

He led me into a rather dark room serving as kitchen and bedroom combined.

On a wicker armchair, placed against the foot of a double bed with a serge cover pulled over it, a young man, his head thrown back, his arms hanging loose, sprawled as if asleep. His distorted features still betrayed his state of shock, and from beneath the disordered and rain-flattened curls of his silky brown hair, a thread of blood trickled down his pale forehead.

I went over. Heavens, it was him! My Florentine poet! My young friend, the one I couldn't get out of my mind!

In the gloom of the large room I hadn't recognised him at first. Quivering with fright and happiness at the same time, and while the forester's wife was holding out my bottle of smelling salts, I used my handkerchief to staunch the blood beading his brow. But since nothing seemed to bring him back to life, I squatted by his knees, overcome with terror, took his limp hands in mine, and I surprised myself, I who had never prayed, by pleading: 'My God, save him!'

Was I afraid, already, of losing a joy I had hardly

possessed? Oh, my happy dream!!

Then I became aware of a change, as if some liquid warmth was beginning to flow through him. A pink flush spread over his cheeks and his drooping eyelids fluttered lightly.

Suddenly he opened his eyes wide. Oh, my friend, those eyes! What wells of tenderness! What stirrings of trust and love in the look he gave me!

It may surprise you, my friend, but a fit of bashfulness came over me, yes, me! And making a violent effort to conceal my confusion, I abruptly stood up.

'Do you feel any better now, monsieur?' I enquired, with convincing nonchalance.

And as if a little ashamed of his weakness: 'Thank you, forgive me' he stammered, 'and if these most kind people could help me back on my bicycle...'

'Wouldn't you rather take advantage of my carriage?' I ventured, encouraged by the forester, who was explaining to him that such a course would be most unwise, and in any case the bicycle in question was in pieces.

Chance had thus engineered an opportunity to be alone with him and I was secretly delighted, I confess. We drove along in the fresh-scented air that follows rain. The bushes and hedgerows sparkled with pearls in the light of the setting sun, and in my soul I felt a deep beatitude, a thing I had never yet experienced.

And he, expression animated and eyes shining, stumbled over himself to express his warm gratitude: I had saved his life; whilst I... jealously preserving this sweet moment, kept silent, fearing that any fulsome words of mine would make him lose his intensity.

After a while we came to a small house, nestled in a thicket of greenery, where he lived with his mother.

'This is it,' he said.

At the same moment Mme Duvert appeared on the steps, beneath an arch of clematis and honeysuckle. Raising a pair of binoculars, she began to scan the horizon anxiously, feverishly, peering in every direction. Then suddenly she let the glasses fall and stared in amazement at the splendid carriage drawing to a halt outside her door.

'Mother!' exclaimed my young friend as, still staggering a little, he clambered down.

It was indeed the woman whose distinguished appearance had already impressed me.

'This is Madame de Valneige, mother. I owe it to her that I'm back here safe and sound.'

And even as she stared wonderingly at me, Mme Duvert, in great agitation, plied us with questions. She wanted to know everything; the three of us were all talking at once.

'But excuse me,' she said, suddenly interrupting the flood of words. 'Let me first of all say how extremely grateful I am, and then won't you please come in. We can get to know one another a little better and we shall be able to talk more comfortably.'

Instinctively I took a step back. One never quite forgets one's beginnings in life. Faint stirrings of my former pureness, memories of little Louise Aubertin from the Touraine rose in my heart, with the result that I was crippled by scruples. How could I possibly deceive this unimpeachable mother, allow my frills to brush against her irreproachable widow's black? Could I breathe the honest air of this peaceful house without choking on it?

So, declining under all manner of pretexts this friendly offer, I got back into the carriage, whilst Paul Duvert followed my departure with a long and troubled gaze.

But no sooner had I returned to my solitude, to my dreaming, than I realised I was a fool, a complete fool!

What on earth was I doing? They had thrown wide the door of this welcoming house, I was being offered a ready-made friendship, the way was clear for me to turn into reality a thing I already dreamed of: seeing Paul Duvert, seeing him often, and, because of an idiotic sense of delicacy, I was closing that door in my own face, and perhaps closing that heart too!

The very violence of my regrets informed me what my feelings really were. It had happened already! The arrow had pierced me! I was in love! I was in love!

I was in love with Paul Duvert. This child, with his frank yet mysterious gaze, his poet's brow, his guileless heart, was something quite new to me, and had strangely disturbed me.

What I felt inside was akin to an illness. If it makes sense to say so, I would call it an exquisite illness, a thing I would have liked to be rid of and wanted to retain, a thing that filled me with fear and with pleasure, which threw me into a panic of fright and hope.

Once again I was trembling at the prospect of reaching out towards a happiness that I have never been able to grasp. Once again I was trembling at the thought of believing for a while only to relapse into doubt!

What makes me think, then, that I shall find in this youthfulness the thing which, in the whole of my career, already lengthy, I have never found? Why should this child, then, be the spark that sets the dry wood ablaze? Why do I think I shall love this Paul Duvert, with his humility, when I am a woman who has remained as marble in the arms of the most brilliant of men? Yes, I told myself all these things, I lectured myself, I made efforts to put it out of my mind, but I was in love, yes I was in love and I was feeling it properly for the first time in my life!

If only he would come, my young hero, if only he would come to me! But would he call on me here? It was true, I had done him some small service, which he would not, perhaps, forget. But on the other hand, Gérard hadn't mentioned that Mme Duvert was such a possessive mother, always anxious, always concerned to guard her son from the pitfalls along life's road. And if, by chance, in spite of her solitary life, she knew the name of Josiane de Valneige, then would that not make me the deepest of pitfalls, the most dangerous, the most to be feared!

And I waited, me, like a convent girl at the first stirrings of her heart consulting the daisies in the fields: he won't come, he will come, he won't come, he will!!!

XV

To the Same

I had been playing this little game for a week and he had not come!

Since I couldn't possibly leave the house, going for walks was out of the question.

I left my blinds down and remained determinedly at home, wandering up and down in a haze of rice powder and drifts of smoke from my Russian cigarettes. One afternoon, towards five, I heard a timid pull at the bell. I don't believe there had been more than ten callers in all my time at Brunoy and I listened with senses alert.

At the same moment, almost as flustered as if it had been for her, Gérard came in to say: 'It's him, madame, it's him!'

'Him, what do you mean...? Someone we don't want to see?'

'No, not at all... it's the young man... you know, M. Paul Duvert, and he's...'

'Gérard, oh my good Gérard! Quick, put my hair up! Quick, my blue dress!' It was important to me to be correct.

And I, who kept the greatest of men waiting, who used to enjoy letting them languish in the anteroom, I was trembling so much I couldn't fasten my dress.

Nevertheless – ah, the power of habit! – before making my appearance, as I stood in front of my dressing mirror, I pulled myself together: I was beautiful, although a little pale; and I entered the drawing room.

M. Paul Duvert was standing over by the wall, bending a little to look at my portrait, you know, the pastel by Gallex. He bowed low in greeting, with a ceremonious gaucheness that was rather sweet, and spoke as if he had learned his speech by heart: 'Forgive me, madame, for coming so belatedly to thank you... a little unwell since my accident...'

'There was no need to thank me,' I told him, extending a hand stiffly. 'I was happy to render you some small service. Let us talk of it no further, if you please.'

The ice was broken, but for a long moment he said nothing more, and neither did I.

The silence, however, was becoming awkward; and, forcing myself to say something: 'Madame your mother is well?' I ventured.

Once we had set foot on the safe ground of mundane politenesses and well-trodden banalities, which often veil deep feeling, sincere emotion, we talked for nearly an hour.

His eyes were alight now, like those banked-up fires where a flame suddenly leaps out, his face was flushed with hopefulness and the rapid chatter that fell from his lips told me a great deal more than he was striving not to tell me...

As for me, I was watching him, radiant, thrilled, never interrupting for fear of breaking the spell of my own joy, when without warning he jumped abruptly to his feet.

'I'm sure it must be getting late... in your company, madame, one forgets the time, and my mother will be waiting for me, growing anxious perhaps. She is so good, my mother!'

'In that case I must not detain you,' I replied, rising with regret. 'But we shall meet again soon, yes?'

And kissing my hand with trembling lips, he lowered his voice to a bare murmur, as if lowering one's voice were tantamount to making a declaration, and said: 'Thank you, until very soon! You make me very happy.'

I do believe Gérard might have been eavesdropping, for she was instantly there on the other side of the door, ready to show him out.

XVI

To the Same

Ah, my friend! I am the happiest of women and the most unhappy: I am in love! I love, I love!!!

Since that visit, I seem to have vaulted the entire distance separating earth from heaven in a single flap of my wings, and in this great leap to have shaken off all the dust that still clung to my feet!

Ah, I understand now what they mean, a simple cottage and its beating heart! But, dreadful to relate, this is the very moment my past comes back to haunt me, it smothers me, as if it was determined to make happiness impossible for me!

To have in my heart a pristine love which my mere breath would tarnish, to be concealing, behind my factitious beauty,

111

uglinesses he knows nothing about, to be almost groaning with misery precisely because I have found at last a long sought after happiness, it is awful, my friend, and it is cruel!

Oh, don't say, 'That poor Valneige, it's all gone to her head again, she's letting herself get carried away, she's in cloud-cuckoo-land.' Don't say, 'This is no different from all the other times, it'll all be over in half a day!' No, no, believe me, I don't want it to be like that, this is something on another scale altogether. This has started a whole new set of strings vibrating inside me, there's a sea-change taking place inside my whole being. I am alive, I feel, I think, I speak, I breathe, I walk, I drink and eat in a totally different way.

Yes, this time I love with the kind of love by which you live or die. And I want to live by it, I do, live by it for a long time, live with all my body and all my soul.

XVII

Jean Leblois to Josiane de Valneige

I am delighted, my friend, by everything I read. Finally! Finally, this could be true happiness! But I have to tell you that there is one shadow over the satisfaction I feel: I am fearful to see you love in such a way someone so young; and fearful of what you have still to tell me. Oh, if only you had been able to keep your feelings under control! That would perhaps have been the wiser course. But I do not feel at all confident. Don't be cross with me for sending futile advice after the event, and believe, as ever, that I am your devoted friend.

    J.L.

XVIII

Josiane de Valneige to Jean Leblois

You're getting old, my dear, you're getting old!

Your excellent, if sleep-inducing advice comes too late.

One does not tell one's heart: Halt!

After being thirsty all my life, do you think, my poor friend, I am not going to drink my fill at the first clear stream I chance on? Do you think that after shivering in my sumptuous surroundings like a penniless creature out on the streets I am not going to wrap myself in comfort and joy at the first caress of the sun?

It would not be human, my good friend; in fact it would be stupid.

Haven't I already amassed, looking back, a sufficient store

of suffering and regret? Didn't I tell you that the other day? So permit me now to glean a few grains, if that's possible, of true happiness in a love that is free from all impurities.

This is life, this is life!

As for that mother, whom I had at first cast as a baleful spirit, I have to say she was not as fearsome as all that. It appeared she was a good woman, gentle and well-disposed even... admittedly, she clearly... didn't know. But rest assured, I did not challenge her love for her son, I was not jealous. He was so obviously a person to be loved, to be adored, that sooner than not love him at all I would have loved him like a mother, like a sister.

You don't understand that, do you? And I don't doubt you're saying to yourself: that's not Josiane talking!

But yes, it is: Josiane transformed, embellished, her soul full of devotion and nobility.

You don't understand that, you men, do you, because your indiscretions and disorderly ways bring no consequences?

Provided you remain honest, decent, generous, it matters very little if you have set tongues wagging, if you have cast hearts and money to the winds with equal abandon, changed your mistress every day, drunk from every cup! No one calls you to account for any of it; and when it suits you, you emerge all shiny and new from those pits of pleasure, those escapades in private rooms and boudoirs to lead some fresh young girl to the altar. You love her, she loves you, and all is for the best in the best of all possible worlds.

But the Suzanne de Colognes, the Mathilde de Courcelles, the Louise Martins and the Valneiges, that's a different matter! And I shall never be in a position to undo what has been done and today, in the dream that I am living, in this love that is regenerating me, this is what is eating at me and killing me.

And yet, my friend, amidst all these miseries, would you believe I had just this one thought, one desire: to see him again!

And so, in the hope of a chance meeting – for lovers, happy accidents are often the way – I rediscovered my earlier passion for roaming the countryside. I spent long hours in Sénart forest, and there, in nature's all-enveloping peace, I would forget, I would hope, I would wait!

To wait in hope for happiness, isn't that already a kind of happiness? And often more reliable!

I had been coming here like this for several days, not at all discouraged at finding myself all alone, with only my dreams for company; when one time...

I had found a comfortable place on a carpet of moss growing thickly under an old oak tree. Nothing could be heard in the silence but the vague stirrings of invisible creatures, flies performing their buzzing quadrilles and, close by, water splashing over white pebbles.

The heat was gradually fading, and among the golden shadows of the setting sun there stole a powerful sense of calm. It stole powerfully over me too, so that I was about to fall asleep and had completely forgotten the good little creature who follows me everywhere, when suddenly I heard in the distance Musette's clear bark and at the same time a sharp and piercing whistle, a sort of alarm signal.

The wood was ringing with this long blast when I saw my Musette dashing back in a panic with a pale brown terrier I vaguely remembered having noticed somewhere, I couldn't recall where. It was dancing round Musette, and growing bolder, when its ears pricked up.

Someone was calling it: 'Moka! Moka!'

It immediately ran towards its master, who was just emerging from a small side path.

It was him! Paul!

He was, I noticed, as startled as I was.

'You here, madame, alone... all alone... in this wood?' he said, hurrying over.

'It seemed so nice here in the calm and cool of the evening, I have lingered longer than I meant. This time of day has a melancholy charm all of its own...'

'Which I have clumsily come along and interrupted, no doubt. Forgive me...'

'Will you feel better if I assure you it is quite the contrary, or better still if I tell you your presence only increases it?'

He looked up at me then, a veiled tenderness in his eyes, and said with a sigh, 'If only it were so, if only it were so...'

'Come along now: if my very makeshift hospitality doesn't scare you off, sit down here with me. There's a little piece of this moss carpet to spare that looks just made for you.'

He didn't need to be asked twice and folded himself at my feet, smiling broadly, as happy as a king.

We chatted like real... friends. I wanted to know everything: I asked about his childhood, his youth, his studies, his favourite things, his ambitions.

He was supposed to enrol at Saint-Cyr military school, his father's long-held hope; but with his health a little delicate, his mother fought against this idea and he had had to abandon it. So he had begun law studies, and he was now aiming to enter the magistracy, to please his mother.

For his own part, he had always liked books and poetry; during classes he used to scribble verses; his mother had found scraps everywhere, in his pockets, under his pillows, in his books and despite all her attempts to deflect him from a path full of nervous upsets, of unhealthy over-excitement and especially disappointment, she had been obliged to allow him, he said, to keep for a mistress... his muse; and he had just, after many setbacks, published a small volume, of which he would be glad to give me a copy.

I listened without interrupting, in a state of dreamy happiness, the way a mother listens to her son, or a woman her lover. I would have liked to go on listening, to let darkness come, the mystery of the woods beneath the star-studded vault, listening to him for ever.

But suddenly the two little dogs, who had run off, reappeared looking suspiciously pleased with themselves and leapt into our laps.

They were made a tremendous fuss of: Paul Duvert praised and petted Musette, whilst I let Moka lick my hands.

"Love me, love my dog," as the English say.

It was charming. But all at once I said, 'Come along, we must get back, it's getting dark. Mme Duvert, I'm sure, is waiting for you, and I....'

'Please, please, just a little longer,' he begged. 'I'm so happy. To hold your hand in mine, and your sweet look making me giddy: would you deprive me so soon of the joys I've always hoped for?'

And taking out, still bloodstained, the little handkerchief I had used to wipe his forehead in the forester's cottage, he said, 'Here, do you recognise this...? I've kept it like a treasured relic. I had a presentiment I was going to love you; and now, today, I love you, I adore you…!'

Oh, my friend, I was moved to the depths of my being!

Our hands sought each other's, fingers clasped fingers, and he laid his head on my knees, overcome with happiness, whilst I, inhaling the soft perfume of his hair, already I was struggling against a mounting intoxication.

Abruptly I rose to my feet; he stood up as well, and without another word between us, we walked side by side along the path that took us back to the edge of the wood.

There, holding hands in a long farewell, and just as we were about to separate, the same words sprang to the lips of each of us: 'We'll come here again!'

And descending darkness shrouded this sweet mystery until the next day.

You are no doubt thinking, my dear friend, that the Josiane you once knew is adopting poetic airs that don't suit her at all.

My God, yes! Even I didn't recognise myself. I was seeing everything in a different light. People, objects, nature were all showing new faces, and I, who had always lived in an alluringly moneyed atmosphere, was now falling into ecstasies over a blade of grass and the twittering of a bird.

What does worry me, on the other hand, is that I'm wearying you and abusing your kindness in reading this. And for that reason I am not going to write to you for a few days. It will allow you a little rest from,

Your old friend, who finds herself terribly shaken by turning over all these memories.

XIX

To the Same

On one of our walks one day, we had gone further than usual and we were walking side by side along the pretty Epinay road, exchanging tender words and savouring the delights of being out in the fresh air, when we noticed coming towards us a pony-trap carrying two men, one stout, the other thin.

'Good day, Josiane!' the stout one said, lifting his arm in a greeting at once familiar and patronising. The eye behind his gold-rimmed monocle winked.

It was that appalling de Raincourt. I must have been under a curse! Just because I had once allowed him through my door, or rather he had forced it, he must pester me for the rest of my life!

In any case, how did this prowler of the boulevards come to be in Brunoy, I ask you!

It was aggravating, I felt tense and on edge, I was casting in my mind for a way to explain his casual manners when Paul Duvert said to me sharply: 'What kind of person is that, the impertinent fellow, daring to greet you in such cavalier fashion? If I knew him…' Then he looked at me intently. 'But you, my friend, you must… know him.'

I became confused, yes, my dear, and went all red.

'No, no… I couldn't say…' I stammered. 'He must have mistaken me for someone. There are so many women with my blonde hair…'

I could see my reply only half satisfied him. He remained thoughtful, wondering, worried, and did not press the matter. But when it came for us to part, he said: 'Will you do me a great favour? When we see each other tomorrow, can it be at your house? There's something too public, too common about the roads, anyone can come along. Sudden encounters upset me, get on my nerves. I feel that if we had some little corner where we'd be on our own, just the two of us…'

'Yes, yes, that's it. Tomorrow,' I said, remembering all at once that we could indeed be on our own. 'Tomorrow at eight.'

For the last two days preparations had been going on in Brunoy for a public entertainment. It was the village fair!

The large square in front of the church was beginning to take on a festive look. Roundabouts and helter-skelters were setting up. A raffle stall was unpacking its arrays of coloured glass trinkets. A fortune-teller of amazing powers, specialising in lovers, robberies and inheritances, was rigging her red velvet tent against the side of her caravan. A tooth-puller was fixing to his cart his advertising display with its gleaming rows of three-franc dentures. The waffle and penny-tart sellers were blowing on their fires like blacksmiths and already a disgusting smell of fried potatoes and paraffin was polluting our pure air. The fair was due to open the following day.

Brilliant illuminations were promised for the evening – probably a few miserable coloured lanterns strung in the trees. But Gérard, brought up exclusively on Paris pavements and never having witnessed a village fair, had dreamed up a scheme with Brunet, the coachman: they would ask Madame permission to go and have a bit of fun and spend the evening taking in the spectacle of the fair.

And since "Madame" wanted nothing better than to have a free hand, those excellent servants were granted all the time they desired, and even a little extra, since with a generosity that left them even more surprised, I gave them until past midnight.

Oh, my friend, the time spent getting ready, waiting for the appointed hour, how delicious! Anyone who hasn't felt it hasn't lived! I took joy in everything. Joy in the dress I was going to put on so that he would find me beautiful, joy in the flowers I had arranged in their vases with my own hands, joy even in listening to the tick-tock of the clock that brought the hour closer, made my heart beat in double measure.

It was real love that I felt for him, then, and what a different feeling it was this time!

And when I thought of the way I used to set the scene back in my days of triumph, the farce I staged for the happiness of others and my own foolish vanity, the layers of make-up I applied to my cheeks, my lips, my heart, I recoiled in disgust, in horror. And this reaction in itself made my love all the greater and dearer to me.

It was nearly eight o'clock in the evening when my old Gérard, all dressed up, came to find me.

'We're going now, Madame, and I came to see if Madame needed anything. Madame has not dined.'

'Yes, I'll have something. Put out some tea and cold chicken in my room, and then off you go, quickly, it's time.'

I had indeed not eaten dinner. In the first place I was not hungry, and then I didn't want them to be late setting off!

So I was alone, quite alone in the house, which had never happened before.

He was coming! I was within touching distance of the happiness I had dreamed of, it was within my grasp; I was going to be able to close my arms round it, embrace it: love, such love!

Screened by the half-closed blinds, I leant at the window. From the baskets of roses and mignonettes exquisite scents filled the air.

It was a fine evening, and in the silence that surrounded me I could hear only the drumming of the wooden horses on the roundabouts, snatches of tunes and the shrill voices of the clowns!

Excellent people, how glad I was they were enjoying themselves!

Suddenly a little squeaking sound came from the gate. I pushed the blind aside a fraction. It was him!

I was trembling so much I could hardly walk to the door to let him in.

Joy makes you terrified!

'At last, at last!' he sighed, holding me tightly.

And, holding hands, we moved towards the large red-tapestried sofa between the windows.

Gazing into each other's eyes, we seemed to be reading the depths of our souls. He knelt at my feet. His whole being quivering with hope and desire, he covered my hands with kisses; and to see the provocative fire in his eyes was like drinking a magic potion.

'I love you so much, Josiane! I love you so much!'

I listened, charmed, enraptured, transported, drinking in these words of love as if I was hearing them for the first time. It was a form of divine music that penetrated to the very marrow of my bones, it was the tremor of new life, it was love.

And the hidden reason behind this ecstasy, my friend, is one you know. People have said to me many times, 'I love you, I adore you.' But however magical those three little words that make the world go round, they had left my heart cold, since I was not in love myself. But how I loved this man!

And yet, would you believe it, I felt a sort of reticence that prevented me from telling him so. Words rose from my heart, burned on my lips, but my love was so real, so pure, so immense that it seemed a profanity to utter now words I had flung about so freely before!

And even as I surrendered to him my feverish hand, even as I felt his own ardour burning ever stronger in myself, I left him to guess the things I was unwilling to say to him.

But suddenly a dark cloud, like doubt, passed across his face.

'You have to tell me, my friend,' he said, abruptly, 'do you really not know the gentleman in the pony-trap at all? I'm curious about him, and I've been finding out what I can. He appears to be a baron, Baron de… de… de… it begins with an R… come on, help me.'

'I told you,' I said, hiding my irritation, 'I do not know him. And why bring up this strange character at a moment like this? Please: leave him be, and let's not talk about it any more.'

And to make a diversion, I briskly stood up.

'Will you make me some tea?' I asked him. 'I haven't mentioned it, but I missed dinner to wait for you.'

A look of joy spread over his face.

'So you do love me a little, my adored Josiane!'

And embracing me with renewed passion, he said with a sigh, 'I'm so happy!'

Gérard had set everything out to perfection.

On a side table, the samovar only needed a match; two chicken wings lay appetisingly in a delicious-looking jelly.

Clearly, love and plain water were not always enough, and my stomach felt horribly empty…!

'What if we made an omelette?' I said. 'It would be fun! We've still got a good two hours, plenty of time to do a little cooking…'

'And some loving,' he added, laughing, to my delight.

He followed me to the kitchen, getting tangled in my long silk train as he tried to stay close, eager to do anything to please me, to satisfy my smallest desire.

The kitchen was gleaming. In the glow of the gas jets, which Gérard had left turned up high, the copper pans shone like golden discs, and the blue and white mosaic of the stove sparkled in its multifaceted glories.

'Now then, let's look for some eggs,' I said, crouching in front of the ancient store cupboard. But whilst I was giving my full attention to exploring the contents of various baskets and bowls, at some cost to my nails, I felt on the back of my neck the warm impress... of a kiss! It was heavenly.

I'd promised to make an omelette. I'd managed to find the eggs, but the butter, where was that? It was Paul who found it.

Playing cooks like this gave us as much pleasure as children holding a dolls' tea party.

For my part, I hadn't done a stroke of housework since the days of little Louise Aubertin; it all seemed very comical to me, and Paul Duvert said he thought my ineptness was adorable.

Triumph at last, it was ready!

Creamy and golden and, bless me, speckled with herbs that we had found already prepared on the chopping board.

Like the Holy Sacrament, Paul carried it into my room.

But we had acclaimed the victory too soon. At the very moment of setting it on the side table, where there was hardly any space left, our dinner slid off its dish, and the omelette... spent the evening on the floor.

And we... we spent it consoling each other with laughter and kisses.

I relate all these trifles from a vanished past to show you how vast and all-encompassing love is if it can be found even in such simple things.

What a good evening! My dream was a reality, and in my soul I felt an opening-out, an overflowing that made me a thousand times happier, for sure, than diamond necklaces and ropes of pearls.

We talked with growing intimacy, leaning close to one another. We planned the times when we would be able to meet, we couldn't carry on without seeing each other.

It was not an easy thing to arrange. Already Mme Duvert seemed suspicious, had begun to question him, or come upon him lost in his thoughts, and he had given thanks for the charming village fair, at which she believed him to be enjoying himself and which had given us this opportunity to be so free.

'But let me assure you, the woman I adore, that nothing will come between us, nothing, and if my mother is not happy…'

These words showed me the full measure of his love. I knew that he adored his mother, that her wishes were his command, and that to be ready to sacrifice them for me, he really must love me.

I pressed his beloved head against my overflowing heart. I put my lips to his hair.

I was mad for him, mad for him! I was about to say: 'I love you, I adore you, I am yours', and once again the words died on my lips.

The key grated in the lock.

Heavens, it was Gérard! It must be midnight then! We had had no sense of time passing.

I ran to intercept her, to tell her… what? I didn't know, my one thought was spare her the all too startling sight of 'the little gentleman', as she called him, in my house at this time of night.

'Wait for me here,' I ordered, as she was entering the kitchen.

Explain this paradoxical situation if you can. Gérard was my confidant, she was almost my friend, she knew everything that went on in rue de Prony, she could name them all, the men who marked like milestones the course of my brilliant life. She had shut the door on one to open it for the next, and now I was playing tricks and concealing things from her!

Even though I acknowledge that her shrewd mind had no doubt guessed my cherished secret already, or that in any case she would know it by tomorrow, I was jealous enough to want to keep it to myself a little longer.

'My friend,' I said, coming back into the bedroom, 'we must separate. It is late, I fear. The hours seemed like nothing to us, time has passed too quickly. You must leave, leave… the better to return.'

'Tomorrow,' he said, and kissed me at length. 'Tomorrow. I love you, Josiane, I adore you. Farewell!'

You are probably thinking, my old friend, that after all these strong emotions and joys, I was only too ready to go to bed, to get some rest. Well, not so! I went over them in my mind, one by one; I savoured them, one by one, for if it is lovely to wait in expectation it is even more lovely to remember and to prolong on one's lips the burning imprint of those kisses.

Until dawn I dreamed at the window, in the scented cool of that beautiful August night, my eyes lost in its starry infinity.

Suddenly, like rockets, two bright lights burst across the sky – two shooting stars.

As you will perhaps remember, lovers have their own little weaknesses, their superstitions. I rapidly made a wish: that I could be his, that he could be mine, and for always!

XX

To the Same

Oh, my friend, what a delirious week! I'd need a whole book to tell you about it.

God, it's wonderful when two people love each other! I had not placed too high hopes on the dream I've pursued all my life, and never have I been as happy as this. And if I have left certain desirable aspects of our love yet to be consummated, it is because one should not spend all one's wealth in one go, and how wealthy I was just at that moment!

He didn't always share my view, he wanted our delight in each other to have no limits, he wanted it all, without reserve or reticence.

'When will you tell me you love me, then?' he would

129

exclaim, squeezing the breath out of me by the force of his embraces. 'Don't you love me, is that it?'

Mad with desire, his gaze wild, eyes blazing, chest heaving, he would throw himself on me with a cry: 'You have to love me! You have to be mine!'

It was torture to resist him, it broke me in two, but I was so afraid – I, Josiane de Valneige – of seeing my happiness crumble through the very act of fulfilling it. The prospect of turning this love into an affair like the others, of seeing it vanish like them after a night of pleasure, a moment of intoxication, repelled me so much that I stiffened in his embrace as if I were defending my life itself.

And while he, burying his head in his hands, would begin to weep like a child, I would tell him very gently: 'Later... love me... I lo...'

Well, no, my dear Jean, I did not say the word quite yet! I waited...! Waited...

XXI

To the Same

Day follows day and no two are alike. After telling you how wonderful it all was, now comes one terrible afternoon that made me feel ill for a long time afterwards.

As on the other evenings, I was expecting him after nine o'clock. At this time of evening it was easier for him to escape his mother's watchful eye, for she retired early. But on this day Mme Duvert was having some friends to dinner and Paul had understood that his presence was essential. So he had come in the afternoon to warn me of this change of plan, which would deprive us of those few hours of happiness.

But as he was coming up the path, guess who it is he finds at my door? That horrible Baron de Raincourt!

Truly, I am cursed!

I was in the drawing room, deep in a book, when Gérard showed them both in.

I suddenly felt quite sick, but put a good face on it nevertheless.

'Delighted to meet you here once again, madame,' the baron said, bending his old spine. 'It's been such a long time...'

'M. Paul Duvert,' I said, introducing him.

And turning to Paul with a determined show of good manners: 'Baron de Raincourt.'

I was hoping these formal politenesses would prevent the baron from going any further.

But he was not to be checked: 'How very unexpected to find you here, my dear Josiane! Do you enjoy living in this out of the way spot? Can you really have left rue de Prony, such a jewel? Because,' he continued, turning to Paul Duvert, 'madame lives in such surroundings there, so artistic, so luxurious...! A home fit for the gods, eh! And I was amazed to think that quiet country lanes... green hedges...'

'But I assure you, baron, that Brunoy is very pleasant,' I said, still trying to disguise my emotion beneath a veneer of civility.

I glanced furtively at Paul. He was deathly pale, his lips were trembling and I could see he was incapable of uttering a word.

The awkwardness was almost tangible and the baron, too much a man of the world not to notice it or let it continue, had the decency to get to his feet.

'I shall leave you, madame... in good company,' he said with a knowing look. 'I am invited to a garden party up at the manor, I must be on my way.'

And falling on the hand I held out to him, he kissed it with exaggerated deference.

'So you lied to me,' exclaimed Paul Duvert, jumping up. 'Didn't you tell me you didn't know him, that ridiculous, worn-out old fop? And today he walks into your house like an old friend. Explain yourself, explain yourself, I have a right to know! I loved you, Josiane... yesterday. Today, I've lost all trust, everything is coming apart.'

'No, no!' I cried in a passion, and took him in my arms. 'No, no, not everything!'

'And what is your love to me, if you have given it to others? What are the kisses on your lips to me if your heart lies somewhere else? I have a right to know, yes, to know about your past, or how am I to hope for any future...?'

'Don't attack me so! I will tell you.'

'Yes, talk to me, talk to me. What sort of person are you who can lie to me like that? What are you hiding?'

He was beside himself with hurt and anger. He frightened me.

'My poor child, calm down,' I said, soothing his head against my breast. 'What woman doesn't have a little history of her own? Now you will learn mine.'

I had a flash of genius.

'I was married once. My husband, a bad man who never, by the way, made me happy, ran off a few years ago with the baron's wife. Where they are now nobody knows, and the humiliated husband has found no better way of taking his revenge than to turn his grotesque attentions on me and make everyone in Paris believe we are in effect a couple. If I told you

I didn't know him it is because, I swear, he has never played any part in my life. As for rue de Prony, I was so miserable there that I think about it and mention it as little as possible… well then, come on! Do you really need to get so upset over any of that?'

How eager for consolation we are when we suffer, how anxious to believe when we doubt!

An adorable smile lit up his dear face. His brow relaxed. And as our eyes instinctively sought each other's, he rediscovered faith and hope.

'Josiane, my Josiane, I do love you. Yes, I can feel it, I have never loved a woman like you. Some have made my heart beat for a moment, excited my senses, but it was nothing but smoke… without fire. You, Josiane, I love you with a love that is lasting and deep.'

And he was so exquisitely tender that I wondered if I wasn't even happier than before.

I also had the relief of thinking that, satisfied by my explanation, he wouldn't harbour such dark suspicions again, and our sky would from now on remain cloudless.

Like a shaft of sunlight after the storm, our restored happiness seemed all the dearer to both of us, and we spent a delicious hour interrupted by kisses, with the anticipation of more to come, by laughter and by renewed protestations of love.

But, as he was leaving, I became aware of a profound change in his features; his eyes had sunk in their sockets and red patches stood out against his unusually pale cheeks.

The recent emotional upheaval, I thought, and I suppressed an anxiety that began to rise in my heart.

XXII

To the Same

A week went by.

'My God, my God! What's wrong?' I began to wonder.

For eight long days I had not seen him. I went through terrible agonies, I formed the most unlikely conjectures, I stopped sleeping at night, I stopped eating, stopped living.

Had the residue of that fatal visit been fermenting in his mind, working on it? Had his heart been assailed by new suspicions? Was he trying to show he was cross with me for my little fabrication so that I would have to love him even more? Oh, God, I just didn't know.

Was he ill perhaps? A fearful anguish gripped me. The other day when he was leaving, his face was drawn, his eyes feverish and his hands damp. And when I thought that I, who adored him, who would have given my life for him, could not run to his bedside if he was ill, that I would be kept away as a stranger!

Oh, my poor Josiane, I told myself, how naïve you were not to make friends with that terrifying mother! You would not now be reduced to such a horrible state of uncertainty and scattered wits, you would be able to see him and look after him perhaps.

In my agitation I came up with the idea of sending Gérard off – she knew everything by now – to collect the village gossip, to try to learn anything. In a small place like Brunoy it couldn't be difficult. I trusted her natural shrewdness: she'd maybe get the greengrocer's wife just along the road to tell her something, the butcher opposite, and certainly contrive an encounter with the woman who ran the 'Berceau d'Anacréon', the village's only inn and a fountainhead of gossip.

I was full of hope, but her investigations went unrewarded. I leant nothing, nothing!

So, like a soul in distress, I took myself off, wandering the countryside. I trod again the paths we had taken together, where I could feel I was breathing his air, stepping in his footprints. I walked past the windows of his house, in the vague hope that some chance sign would give me a clue; but there again, nothing! The blinds on the little house were pulled half way down.

And I was slowly making my way back home, broken in body and spirit, walking in a fog like a drunkard, when I suddenly came across an old woman and my attention was caught by her disreputable clothes, garish and dirty at the same time.

Deep-set grey eyes which seemed to penetrate the depths of your soul peered from her wizened face and her beaky nose, prominent chin and thin lips suggested a forceful character, a powerful will.

'The summer of life... ah, my beauty, the age of storms,' she murmured in strange, prophetic tones as she passed.

Startled, I stopped and stared at her.

'*Past, Present And What Is To Come:* how about it, fine lady? Costs very little... take advantage while you can!'

She had chanced on fertile ground: my emotions were in such a state that this vulgar fortune-teller seemed like an oracle to me.

Yes, yes, she had materialised on this very spot for the express purpose of bringing me enlightenment: through her agency I would know everything. I didn't hesitate for a moment.

'Will you visit me at home in one hour's time?' I said. 'You can see the house there, on the right, with the tall gates, that's the one.'

And the old woman, her grey eyes flickering, made some arcane sign and whispered: 'In one hour!'

I warned Gérard, who would certainly have sent this ragged old woman packing, a leftover from the fair – and I waited.

She arrived an hour later.

For this consultation, the old woman had combed her tousled grey hair, her face was less dirty and a brand new red scarf covered her collapsing bosom.

'Come in,' I said. 'Come in. What do you need?'

'A bit less daylight,' she said, looking towards the blinds, 'a table, a chair and that's all.'

I arranged these things as best I could, and when we were seated in the mysterious semi-dark she required, 'Now then,' she said, 'I work with the cards. Do you want the little pack or the full one?'

'The full one, the full one!' I exclaimed. 'And tell me everything, everything!'

She drew from under her red scarf an enormous bundle of cards, weird and bizarre, elaborately decorated, grimy where fingers had left their marks and which gave off an odour... that I will not attempt to describe.

Should I confess, my dear Jean, my emotions were at fever pitch, I was shaking, I was hardly breathing for fear of missing what she might be thinking and above all what she was about to say.

She lined up her cards with every sign of joy, as if she took pleasure in seeing happy circumstances in them, her small eyes blinked with satisfaction, and after a moment of solemn stillness: 'Oh, a wonderful life!' she cried. 'Loves, riches, fame, it's all there. And you've been adored in your time, haven't you just! On top of that, such beauty too! All the same, here's a nine of spades that niggles me. Hum, let's see... well, yes, something we're still missing in spite of it all? Cupid not playing fair, eh! So much for the past!'

And after shuffling the cards and getting me to cut them with my left hand – the heart's hand: 'Let's look at now,' she said. 'Ah, yes! It's going well, it's going well. I see you happy and fulfilled. You've found your dream, you're madly in love, and he loves you, how about that!'

I was listening to her open-mouthed, the old flatterer.

So far she had got everything so exactly right I was ready to believe whatever she might say about the future.

But she suddenly frowned, her face went dark again, and mumbling who knows what diabolical formulation, she made the sign of the cross and fell silent.

'Heavens, what is it?' I said, genuinely impressed. 'A misfortune, an accident? Tell me, speak up…'

Her hesitation was a torture in itself.

'Come along now, what is it?' I demanded impatiently. 'I said I wanted to know everything.'

'Well then, I see darkness, that's what it is. Darkness… darkness.'

'He's going to die!' I cried. 'He's ill… this is no good. Here you are. There's twenty francs, you're nothing but an imbecile.'

And darting her little grey eyes towards the glinting gold coin: 'Patience, good lady. You will have your triumph… the women you count as enemies…'

Ah, my friend, don't make fun of me! I was so unhappy!

And see how bizarre the human heart is. All the time that old witch had been telling me things I found agreeable, I had considered her amazingly gifted and clairvoyant! And as soon as she predicted misfortunes I didn't want to contemplate because they tore my soul apart, I called her an imbecile.

And yet, in spite of myself, I was obsessed, haunted…! Darkness…! Darkness…!

XXIII

To the Same

My friend, I was still in the same state when I had a day of such emotional turmoil that the blow it dealt felt mortal. And if I find the strength to describe it to you here it is because, in spite of everything, talking to you about one's sufferings helps ease the heart.

You will tell me no doubt that I am a woman who exaggerates despair as much as she exaggerates love. How could it be otherwise when they go hand in hand?

The day was torrid, the heat overwhelming. Careless of anything else, my mind taken up with him alone, my thoughts adrift in the vastness of my love, of my anxiety, I was resting on my chaise longue, hair loose, and in a state of personal disorder that closely matched the disarray of my heart when, suddenly, there before me I saw – whom? Mme Duvert.

Her face was exceptionally pale, her expression haggard, her step unsteady. My difficulty in recognising her at first was accentuated by the sheer surprise of her visit.

'Forgive me, please, madame,' I said, ashamed to have been discovered – by her especially – in my flimsy garments, 'forgive me for receiving you in this state.'

'It is of no importance,' she said, with ill-disguised disdain. 'A serious matter has arisen, so serious I am compelled to visit you in person. But when one is a mother, one finds the courage, one accepts any humiliation.'

'What do you mean, madame?'

'I have spent nights with no sleep, days with no rest, agonising over this visit, caught between desire and fear. Three times I got half way and turned back, until, worried out of my wits and galvanised by the hope of saving my son, I have bridged the chasm that separates us.'

'I am less and less clear what it is you wish to say,' I replied in a haughty manner that ill-suited me no doubt. 'And the tone in which you choose to address me, madame…'

'My God, enough. Let's put our cards on the table. It is unnecessary to pretend. You love my son. He loves you. And this love is killing him!'

'This is a strange reproach, to say the least. Is it my fault that chance threw us together? Do you blame me for being of assistance to your son?'

'Far from it,' she said, softening a little. 'But you have upset his life, upset his health, upset his happiness… and mine. There are many sorts of love…'

'What do you know of that?'

'There are many sorts of women…'

'You insult me, madame…'

'Don't stand on your dignity, we shall never come to an understanding. Just hear me out. A week ago I had a mortal shock: my poor son began to spit blood. I know this disease, I witnessed its deadly progress. His father…'

Oh, my dear Jean, a dagger went through my heart! Something ripped inside me, I turned horribly pale; but I didn't interrupt, I let her keep talking.

'Absolutely terrified, I rushed to Paris, to talk to my brother, to see my doctor and arrange an immediate examination. In the evening we were all gathered as a family, everyone concerned by the deterioration in my son's condition. I told the story of the bicycle accident, observing that his health had noticeably weakened after it, and I mentioned, meaning to speak of you in the warmest terms, your name.

'"Mme de Valneige! Josiane de Valneige!" my nephew interrupted. He's a fine-looking young man but a little too fond of the fashionable world. "That's not possible, aunt. She's one of the most lionised women of the day, everyone wants her. One of the richest women in all of Paris going off and burying herself in Brunoy? Who's ever heard of Brunoy? It doesn't exist! You must be making a mistake. In any case, I pity poor Paul, however flattered he may feel, if he's fallen into her clutches. A woman like that will finish him off in no time!"'

Oh, my poor Jean, I can't tell you how terrible it was! I crumpled, head in my hands, chest racked with great sobs that I couldn't hold back any more. I hardly heard all those bitter words, I could only feel one thing: they were going to take him away from me, he was ill, I could lose him.

And hot tears such as I had never wept before fell between my fingers on to my crumpled dressing-gown.

Then she was the one who consoled me.

'You truly love him then,' she said, taking my hand. 'Poor woman…! But what about me? Consider this: he is my one and only joy, my one hope. Think how alone I am in the world. It would kill me if he were to die!'

'And do you think it wouldn't kill me too?'

And with a groan that wrenched at my heart, she said again: 'You really love him then, you really do love him…!'

For a long while we sat there, overwhelmed, not saying a word. A silence of the dead hung between us!

She was the first to break it, joining her hands in ardent entreaty.

'Tell me you won't try to steal my son from me,' she said. 'My Paul whom I adore…! It will be easy enough for a woman like you to forget him.'

Well, my friend, I stiffened like a tigress at the insult, anger flushing my cheeks.

'Do you think women like me don't have a heart like you, then? Do you think nothing in here is any good, the love we feel can't be just as noble and pure?'

'Then I beg you, prove it to me, and sacrifice yours to mine. God will count it in your favour.'

'But he loves me too! He loves me! Don't you realise?'

'Yes, I know,' Mme Duvert replied in a hushed voice and with some effort. 'Poems addressed to you, a letter to you begun but not finished because of his illness. I confess, I couldn't help glancing at it. But I didn't yet know…'

'So then!' I cried, at the end of my tether, in the grip of appalling fear, 'If he is to be saved, what must be done? What do you want me to do?'

'Stop loving him… at least stop telling him so… don't try to see him any more.'

'That is impossible, madame, impossible! Do you think we can uproot love from our hearts like weeds in the fields? Do you think that when one has found a treasure it is a simple thing to hand it over…! What if I told you, as a woman who has been greatly loved in her life, that this is the first time I have ever loved anyone myself? That my life has been regenerated by this young and pure love, that I have been made a better person? Maybe then you would feel pity for me too at the prospect of losing him! I beg you in my turn: don't take him away from me! Since it must be so, I will be his sister, his friend, I will watch over him, like you the best of mothers, and we will love him and cherish him together, the two of us. But if I do make this sacrifice, swear to me that if your anxieties were to increase… that if he grew worse, you would let me come to him.'

Mme Duvert remained thoughtful.

I looked at her. The tight features relaxed a little, a look of pity came into her eyes, and tears were not far behind.

'If what you are promising is not beyond your strength to keep, if you will remember that my poor child is ill, that strong emotions could kill him, then,' she said with resignation, 'I place it in God's hands. You will see him again. I put my faith in you, you will not break my trust.'

And as she was leaving, making her halting way towards

the door, I said in a wave of deep feeling: 'I promise… but he, at least, must never know.'

So all of this was another of destiny's traps, then, and in its cruelty, what a refined one! To put happiness in my hands only to snatch it back, to let me touch the reality of my dream only to make me feel its loss more bitterly! I could have died from grief!

Then I began to disbelieve it all, I told myself that it was not possible, that in order to prise him away from me this mother – women of my sort are always fatal in the eyes of mothers – had no qualms about saying he was sicker than he was, and that I was thoroughly naïve!

But no, her despair was real: had I not seen her wet eyes and her twitching fingers when she told me: 'My son has been spitting blood!'

And had the fortune-teller not seen in her cards darkness… darkness… darkness!

I could feel it, I was going to lose him, he was going to die!

XXIV

Jean Leblois to Josiane de Valneige

My poor Josiane! My poor friend, I can tell you are in great distress and this is only the beginning.

And it has come as a shock to me too, a blow to the heart.

The sadness of life, the sadness of what fate has in store, alas! How marvellous this love of yours was and what a joy it should have been to you!

Now, thinking of you, Josiane, I have before me the poignant image, roles reversed, of the Lady of the Camellias: and yet I think your heart was torn even more than hers! Those who are left behind, are they not the ones most to be pitied?

XXV

Josiane de Valneige to Jean Leblois

Alas, alas, it was truly terrible!

After a month of separation, the poor child came to see me again. I had given up expecting him.

What a change, my friend! What a sad contrast in the way this clear-browed twenty-year-old approached me, wearing a shawl round his shoulders, dragging himself towards me like an old man! His back had become bent, his chest hollow, and in his pinched features and pale cheeks only his eyes retained their living intensity, their warm flame of love!

'Oh, my darling!' he said, throwing himself into my arms. 'It wasn't being ill that made me think I might die, it was not seeing you. What long days of torture! The suffering, the fever, the sleepless nights, that was nothing, Josiane. But waiting for the woman you love, telling yourself you might close your eyes for ever without seeing her dear smile again, without giving her a last kiss, that, can you see, is to die a thousand deaths! There were several times when I was on the point of confessing everything to my mother – she is so good! – several times when I very nearly called out to her: "If you want me to get better, let the woman who is my whole life come to me!" And each time, some feeling of awkwardness I can't describe made me hesitate, the words died on my lips. Today, you are mine, I am here, pressed against your heart, and nothing else, nothing…'

At that moment a fit of dry, hollow coughing shook his frame and a cold sweat appeared on his forehead.

'It's nothing,' he said, barely able to speak and falling back into an armchair. 'I'm still a little weak.'

Poor friend, in his joy at seeing me again he had not noticed the coldness of my demeanour, the kind of reserve I had imposed on myself as a consequence of my promise. But as he slowly recovered his breath: 'Well, Josiane!' he said sadly. 'Are you not glad to see me then? Is that all it takes, a few days' absence, being removed from your sight, and already I'm removed from your heart?'

Oh, how they wounded me, those bitter words! The reproach stirred a silent rebellion in my soul.

What? I would have given my life for him. Here I was, filled with a wild longing to throw my arms round him, to give myself to him entirely, and I was not allowed to tell him so. This time my role was to pretend indifference, when so many times in the past I had had to pretend the opposite!

But what had she thought she was asking of me, that mother of his? What sort of love did she mean? How can you play games like this when you are young, when you are in love with each other, when everything is so vivid inside you?

And already at the first test the promise which she had forced from me, the sacrifice I had offered in a moment of high emotion, was near to bending. Would I be capable of keeping it?

But he had remained very pale, in a state of inert misery that filled me with alarm.

I felt convinced that a tender word, an embrace, would warm and revive him and I was about to tell him, 'But I love you, I adore you!' – when I remembered: I had given my word!

So it was decreed that the words that burned inside me could never be said! Until now, I had held them back from a reluctance brought about by the very strength of my love; today, it is a dreadfully cruel oath that checked them on my lips.

Therefore I turned my lover's love into a sister's and mother's love, and allowing my passion, my sensual longing to be overruled by a near-sublime sense of devotion, I gently crossed over to where he sat and placed a kiss on his forehead.

'Are you not perhaps a little chilly near that window?' I asked, rearranging on his shoulders the shawl his mother had no doubt placed there. 'What I want to do is look after you, make you better.'

And, calling Gérard, I had her bring him a cup of warm milk, which, to please me, he was obliged to accept, whilst I took his long hand, now thinner than ever, between mine.

For a short time, at least, I was able in this way to allay his suspicions. But what a huge effort it took me to play my role with any conviction!

Can you imagine, my dear Jean, the dazzling Josiane reinvented as a Sister of Charity? And yet there was an unexpected sense of joy, a secret sort of pleasure in my own suffering. I experienced a novel sense of pride; I felt like a person I had never been.

He seemed a little happier, calmed and contented. Now he described how his illness had suddenly come on, his poor mother's terror, the letter he had begun to write but been unable to finish, the long days of boredom and worry, the doctor's visits, the battles he had fought to be allowed to leave the house and come to me, how he had guessed my anguish, the prolonged torture of a separation which redoubled his own suffering by adding mine.

And then he wanted to know how I too had endured the strain, if I had thought about him through the days, through the nights, in the mornings and in the evenings; if I loved him less, if I loved him more; if I had wept, suffered.

And so the hours fled by in these sweet exchanges.

The sun was already setting, and the freshness in the air felt all the cooler for the day's strong warmth.

'I'm going to send you home, my dearest friend,' I said firmly. 'We must be careful. This is your first time out. Hurry back now. We have happy times ahead of us.' And I continued: 'Why don't we meet again tomorrow, in our forest, at our special place? The open air will do you good and it will be delightful.'

I could see my suggestion did not much appeal to him.

Coming to my house, where we could enjoy an easier

intimacy, had always seemed to him preferable. It was a better way to be together, just the two of us, he said! Poor child, he couldn't understand that it was precisely to be less together, the two of us, alas, that I had been resolute enough to suggest going to a place where anyone might pass and where an unexpected encounter, a surprise of some sort, necessarily put us on our guard.

Poor friend, how he would have pitied me if he had been aware of my sacrifice, instead of accusing me, no doubt, of loving him less than before, when in fact I loved him too much!

The next day, we were due to see each other at three o'clock, in the woods.

XXVI

To the Same

The night was dreadful, full of lowering dreams, of nightmares; and looming before me like the ghost of my happiness, the wasted face, the pale brow of that poor child. No, no, I couldn't believe it, and, crushed beneath the rubble of my hopes, I was left without strength or courage.

And yet, there he was, expecting joy and smiles from me; there he was, opening his arms to me, wishing to share his life with me. How was I to appear happy before him when I had death in my soul? How, above all, was I to appear cool and detached when the fiery look in his eyes was itself enough to ignite ardours more powerful than I had ever known?

What a struggle, what a terrible struggle! What on earth

had I been doing, promising a thing I could not do?

What must I do now, then, since this love was killing him!

And Mme Duvert's words rang in my ears with their bitter irony: 'Stop loving him!'

That was impossible, and if, through the very power of my love, I had finally been strong enough to hide it from him; if, to outward appearances, I had indeed made a sacrifice of it, then wouldn't my cold attitude have itself been the surest spur to his own love, and the most dangerous?

Well... if, to cure him of it, it had been necessary to confess I was unworthy of him, that his heart had taken a wrong turning, that he had been in love with none other than the Valneige woman...! Well yes, if, to save his life, that sacrifice had been necessary, I would have made it; and gathering up like precious wreckage the remains of my shattered love, I would have let myself die of it, withering away, as he was dying, from the dreadful consumption that was eating away at him, hollowing him out.

The heart is strange. In my suffering, I experienced a fierce desire to return to the place where I had been happy: the mossy carpet by the oak tree where, in the warm stirrings of spring, he had first told me he loved me. Oh, how joyful it had all been then!

I was the first to arrive. Although it was a fine October day, there was already a certain melancholy in the air, and little autumnal gusts blew the yellow leaves about. The tree was half bare, and the moss, scorched by summer's heat, was strewn with dead twigs.

And there, as I set myself to wait, the full measure of my grief broke over me, coursing through me, if I may speak of it this way, like a sensual wave.

Suddenly I caught a slow tramp of feet in the rustle of dead leaves covering the ground. I stood up, fixed a smile on my lips and walked towards where the footsteps were coming from. It was surely him.

Yes, it was my poor little Paul Duvert, trailing sadly along, his plaid shawl still wrapped round his shoulders. He looked like a convalescent, his face was pale and tired, but his eyes as full of brilliance as ever.

'Ah, my beautiful beloved!' he said, coming up to me. 'There are so many things I have to tell you today, my head is buzzing with plans, I couldn't wait to see you.'

When we had settled side by side he put his arm round me and held us tightly together.

I let him talk.

These first days of autumn had made him very sad to begin with. They seemed to threaten a separation, he had wondered if I might want to return to Paris. Then he had remembered that I had once talked with enthusiasm of the charms of a winter spent in Nice and he had put all this together and formed a plan.

Every cloud has a silver lining: he would arrange to be sent to Nice to complete his recovery! His mother, he knew, was ready to do anything. Then I would come and join him, and we would live the life of sweet selfishness we had dreamed about so long, the two of us together. And his cherished project did not stop there – the projects sick people devise to delude themselves! In the spring, when he would be restored to health, we would walk down the aisle of Brunoy's little church, under the warm caress of a new season, to have official blessing on a love that could only bring pleasure to his mother!

'For you belong to me, Josiane. For you will be my wife.'

Ah, my dear friend, I was overcome. It was too much!

Poor woman, what was I to think? And him, poor child!

But what would you have had me do? Dash his hopes with a single word, when his hopes were perhaps the only things keeping him alive? Burst out suddenly with: 'No, no, I am not worthy of you, love me no more, forget me'? – I didn't have the courage.

And in the sombre glow of the setting sun, as I looked into his sickly and radiant face, I said to myself: Let it go; why would I rob him of his dearest and perhaps his last illusions?

At that moment a stronger gust of wind sent leaves spinning along the peaceful lanes.

'Let's go back quickly,' I told him, 'or you'll be unwell again.'

'Leave you, my darling Josiane! Not yet, not yet. Let me enjoy the exhilaration of being in your arms a few moments more. Let me, let me…'

He was becoming so pressing I could feel my resolve about to waver. It was so painful to be forever deflecting his bursts of passion, constantly putting a brake on his flights of eloquence! But, making a great effort, I stood up, took command of the situation and said, in a playful tone: 'A lover goes where his loved one leads.'

'To your house, then? Yours, my Josiane?'

'Tomorrow, yes… yes, tomorrow.'

And reluctantly he took the path home.

XXVII

To the Same

I had had a kind of presentiment that he would not come. He looked so tired when we parted. Who could say if he hadn't caught a chill, or if, when the evening wind got up, it hadn't done him some irreparable harm?

A long week went by. The torture of separation and anxiety began all over again. There was no doubting it this time: he was ill, he could even be dying; I could not rush to his side and no one summoned me!

I fell into such a state of collapse that my angelic Gérard grew alarmed.

'Have you heard anything?' I asked her.

And she told me that a carriage had been hired at the

'Berceau d'Anacréon', that very morning, to meet at the station a famous doctor from Paris. That poor little Duvert was much worse, his lungs were failing... the time of year, all the leaves coming down... Mme Duvert was very upset, she wouldn't survive, she adored that son of hers...

'Leave me,' I cried, distraught, 'I need to be alone, leave me.'

But I adored him too, and was I to stay here, separated from him, in mortal anguish? I could hear him calling out to me in his agony! I could see the light going out in those beautiful eyes that had so disturbed my life. A hundred times I pictured him dying, thinking I was dying too.

And there I remained, in this extreme distress, harbouring jealous thoughts about that mother who didn't love him the way I did and who had him all to herself, held him even now in her arms.

Uncertainty and torment make evil counsellors. Insensibly, without our noticing, they drive us towards reckless, strange decisions, make us lose sense of what we can and can't do. We no longer see objections to anything; everything becomes possible, we find an excuse for anything.

And that is how, in my dreadful anguish, an idea entered my head like a flash of lightning. I could go and wait at the station, catch the wise doctor summoned to my beloved's sickbed, of whom Gérard had just spoken. He was the man who could give me proper news, and then I would know something.

And why not, then? I would tell him that I'm a relation, a friend, come to that even the truth. And while asking him to keep my request a secret, I would beg him to keep nothing from me. What could be more natural?

And without further hesitation, I put on my hat and made my way determinedly to the station.

It was eleven o'clock as I arrived.

Outside, by the wicket fence, a carriage was waiting, all newly polished.

'What time is the next train from Paris?' I asked the first railway official I met.

'In twelve minutes,' he said.

I didn't have long to wait, thank God, since it was only this dreadful nervous agitation that had brought me here.

Oh, my dear Jean, those twelve minutes seemed like a century to me. I paced the platform from one end to the other, bumping into porters, into trunks being pushed on trolleys, my eyes distracted by the hosts of bright-coloured posters and railway maps, hardly taking in what I was seeing, and my ears filled with the sound of whistles as if there was always a locomotive just behind me.

In Brunoy's little station, people must surely have wondered if that poor lady wouldn't be better locked up!

At last, the train from Paris!

The doors opened. People dashed forward, risking a broken neck to gain an extra minute. Baskets and parcels were hastily unloaded, all the small fry of luggage. People met people, exchanged greetings, embraced each other. As for me, I stared all round in search of a gentleman who might resemble a doctor. I had a mental picture of what a prince of science must certainly look like… dignified in posture, affable in manner, greying hair and at the very least a scrap of ribbon in his buttonhole.

No one fitted my man's description closely, or in any way

at all.

I looked over towards the carriage; it was still waiting however. So, bravely, I went up to the driver.

'Is this carriage free?' I said, as if I wanted to hire it.

'No, madame,' came the answer. 'I'm waiting for an important medical doctor arriving on the express in five minutes, if it isn't late, as usual.'

'So what was the train that just went through?' I asked.

'A local train, madame.'

Sure of not missing my doctor this time, I went to sit down in the waiting room for a moment to recover my composure.

But soon a din even louder than the first threw the peaceful little station into a flurry. This time, it was the express.

Only one passenger alighting at Brunoy!

My doctor surely: it could only be him.

Can you imagine my amazement when I recognised the doctor as an old acquaintance of mine!

One switches so easily back to hopefulness that this happy coincidence poured balm on my heart, and I told myself, just because it was him, that he was going to bring off a miracle and save my poor Paul.

After the first expressions of astonishment at running into each other again, I said to him: 'Ah, dear doctor! Can you give me a few moments? There's something I have to ask you, something that means a great deal to me.'

He looked, I must say, somewhat irritated. A patient was waiting for him; time was pressing. But when I insisted and pronounced the name of Paul Duvert, he stopped short and said: 'I am at your disposal.'

And we went into the waiting room.

159

'Dear, dear doctor,' I said without preamble, 'I'm going to confess all. This poor child you've come to save from death's clutches, I'm in love with him. I beg you, cure him for me!'

'Well now!' he said with his good-natured laugh. 'Madame de Valneige's latest adventure! That's what you mean by coming out to the country for a rest, how funny. Well, never mind…! It's not serious, at least…'

So forcefully did I make clear that the opposite was the case, and in my pleadings he recognised such genuine grief, that he was moved by my plight.

'You won't, will you,' I said then, clasping my hands, 'you won't keep anything from me; and you will, won't you, tell his mother she mustn't obstruct him in any way, that if he asks to see me she'll send for me… this young man is in love with me too!'

The good doctor was doubtless saying to himself he had stumbled into a very annoying situation here, that I had become completely scatty; and yet he promised not to return to Paris without letting me know what was happening.

'I'm going back on the twelve forty train,' he said, 'and if you care to wait for me here again…'

And the carriage carried him off at full tilt.

I didn't feel I had the strength to go home, and I began to wander round the little square adjacent to the station, stopping at frequent intervals to sit on the benches because my heart was pounding so hard.

God, how cruel it felt, and long, waiting like this! What was this worthy doctor going to say to me? What would his diagnosis be? Would it be a death sentence, or would he give me back a little hope?

Alas, alas, I didn't need to question him! His expression was sombre and worried, as if all his knowledge had been useless.

'You wish me to keep nothing back, my dear child. Well…'

'Is there no hope?' My breath came so unevenly, I could barely speak.

'None,' he said, simply. 'It's too late to try anything.'

And, squeezing his hand with enough strength to crush it, I fled to weep at home.

His death sentence was pronounced, then! My God, my God, he was lost, lost for ever to me, I was not going to see him again!

But… this mother, did she not, in return for my promise, make me a promise too? And if I have kept mine, now is the moment, Mme Duvert, for you to keep yours: you said I would see him again…

We are brought together by a shared grief; it is not about the Valneige woman any more, it is about the woman who has been in love with your son!

And while emboldened by these sentiments, I quickly seized pen and paper and addressed to my poor friend's mother a few lines asking her to receive me.

Pity me, my dear Jean: I was cruelly left for three long days without news.

I was ready to do anything. I was as fully prepared to face the wrath of this pitiless mother, to test her vigilance, as I was to throw myself at her feet and beg permission to visit him.

In this state of torture, I was wondering if my agony could possibly last any longer, when Gérard, looking most surprised, brought in to me the visiting card of 'Abbé Bonavent.'

It was a considerable shock. No priestly robes had ever crossed my threshold.

But I understood... he was coming to tell me, all too probably, that the end had come... that my poor Paul... wild with grief, forgetting I was about to address a man in holy orders, I stumbled to the drawing room where he was waiting.

'He's dead, isn't he? He's dead!' I burst out, unable to hold back my tears.

'Calm yourself, madame, I beg you, calm yourself,' the worthy man said, in a voice both kindly and authoritative. 'It is at times like this that we need all our courage. As you have guessed, I have come to you as the envoy of the very unfortunate Mme Duvert, an old friend whose request I cannot refuse... which will explain...'

'...how it is that you, monsieur l'abbé, come to find yourself in the home of Josiane de Valneige... I understand.'

'Just so,' he added swiftly, with visible relief. 'And therefore, my poor child, I shall speak to you without circumlocution. I know everything. Therefore do not be afraid to bare your heart to an old man, a minister of God who is familiar with every error and every weakness, but also knows how to forgive and to pray.'

And I allowed him to talk on, as if I would find in his words of charity the courage to bear what he was about to tell me.

Eventually, unable to hold back any longer: 'Monsieur l'abbé,' I said, 'be merciful, do not hide things from me. Is he still alive? Is there no hope? Has he not spoken my name? Has he not asked to see me? He loved me so much...! Won't you answer, monsieur l'abbé? He is dead, isn't he? Yes, he is dead!'

'Alas! Yes, the poor child's sufferings are over,' the priest said, his eyes damp. 'Pity that mother, madame. Pity that mother, who had no one else in the world.'

'And what about me?' I cried in a violent surge of emotion. 'Don't you think I am to be pitied? Don't you think I am suffering? Death ends everything, monsieur l'abbé, and yet Mme Duvert did not keep her promise. I was supposed to see him again. She had made me a promise, she had sworn to send for me at the final moment.'

'Sometimes death surprises us, madame...

'Be resigned, be full of hope, and may your suffering be the first stage on the road to a new life. As you know, much shall be forgiven those who have greatly loved. Farewell, madame, farewell.'

And he left me, shaking my hand in fatherly fashion.

He was gone, then, my poor Paul; so I would never see him again!

And so she had not kept her promise, Mme Duvert, a promise that was nevertheless a sacred one! I had faithfully kept mine; and it had surely cost me more than it would have cost her to keep hers. What had I asked of her, great God! To let me see for one last time this boy whose very breath contained my own life; to let me say to him before it was too late: I love you! And harshly, inexorably, with no pity for anyone's grief but her own, she had kept me away!

I was not the one, my darling Paul, to see the last glimmer in your eyes; I was not the one to feel the last beat of your heart. But was I not the one who loved you the most? Oh, hideous, hideous regrets!

More than an hour had gone by since Abbé Bonavent had

left and I hadn't moved.

I was still there, crushed, the immensity of my distress preventing all rational thought, when I noticed the gathering dusk: it would soon be dark.

There came over me then an irresistible urge to be close to him, wherever that was, however I might manage it. So, swaying like a drunkard under the influence of my grief, but believing in my madness that I could still save something from this shipwreck, I took advantage of the twilight (you know what I mean, don't you?) to take the road to the little house from which I had been excluded.

Six o'clock was striking from the tower of Brunoy's little church. Wrapped in a long cloak and with a thick veil concealing my pinched face, I set course, though I barely had the strength to walk upright, for the little house in Sénart forest. The only true joys I had known, the hopes I had held most dear, here was where they had lived and here, little by little, in the peace and silence, they were dissolved into nothingness.

I thought that the whole world must be weeping with me, that a long mourning veil lay over all of nature and that all busyness, everybody's lives, must come to a halt here because inside poor Josiane everything was broken.

But no, men and women passed on their way, their indifference only emphasising my horrible torment, and nothing in the neighbourhood of that devastated dwelling showed any sign of the drama that had reached its climax there.

Then my head began to clear and I thought: What did I imagine I was going to do when I got there, for heaven's sake? I wasn't going to be able to see him. I was out of my mind...

But all the same, yes: I would learn something at least.

The glow of a light might show me where he lay, I would be closer to him, I… oh God, I didn't know. But I walked, I kept on walking, until at last, ready to drop, I arrived outside the gate.

For a long minute I stood where I was. Everything was dark, as dark as death. Two windows alone showed a wavering light behind their lowered blinds. There, no doubt, in the funereal gleam of the candles, my beloved slept. My temples throbbed, my heart pounded as if ready to burst. My grief was so acute it came as a physical pain. I almost lost my head and began to wonder if I shouldn't simply ignore the hostility or anger of this cruel mother, walk into her house anyway and clasp in one final embrace the being I had so adored – and the one person I had been unable to tell!

But no, I could not destroy the sanctity of this supreme moment. How could I kneel at the foot of that death-bed and pray in silence when all was stormy revolt inside me?

But another thought suddenly leapt into my whirling head.

Mme Duvert, abbé Bonavent had told me, wished to inter her unhappy son in the family vault they had at Père-Lachaise, and, before his final journey, he would pass the night in Brunoy's little church, where his body would be taken by the few friends they still knew.

What if, maybe, I could obtain permission to pray at his side! What if I, who had been kept at arm's length from his bed of suffering, without compassion or regard for my profound love, what if I could pass this last night alone with him! Yes, it would bring a measure of release from my extreme grief to leave before this altar of death the shards of my forever-broken heart.

Obtaining this favour, this mercy from abbé Bonavent became a fixed idea, an obsession. I had not failed to discern, beneath his priestly gravity, a degree of sympathy and good will. I would go and find him; he would take pity on me.

Ah, my poor Jean, how my heart was trembling when, the following day, after a sleepless night, I made my way to the modest presbytery. I found the worthy priest walking in his little garden, reading his breviary. I could not pretend that the expression of pained surprise that passed over his face escaped me; and even though it was from the very depths of my suffering that I had summoned it, I could feel my confidence failing.

However, when he had ushered me into the humble little office where he had many times, no doubt, welcomed tortured and unhappy souls with kindness, I found my courage somewhat restored.

'Monsieur l'abbé,' I began, hands joined in supplication, 'I come to you, who must surely be as merciful as God himself, to ask if you will grant me a favour, just one. I am in such distress!'

'What can I do for you, my child? Speak.'

And so, encouraged by his gently compassionate tone, his expression of genuine goodness, I continued: 'Oh, Father! All the meaningless clamour of this life fades to silence at your feet. What I am about to ask, if I dare, may perhaps appear sacrilege to you. But you are the representative of goodness and mercy. Allow a suffering woman to approach the sanctuary of Peace and Forgiveness. I will feel grateful with my whole being; but more than that, I feel my soul will rise to a higher plane through you, through the Christian charity you bestow on my grief… allow me to be near my poor friend one last time, let me say my last farewell, let me keep vigil over him in the crypt where he is to be laid. You know, monsieur l'abbé, I was promised that I should see him again and I did not see him! For pity's sake, I beg you, grant me in recompense this supreme favour…'

For a long time he sat silent, forehead creased in thought, as if a little unsure what to say; but, I could see, quite affected.

'Poor woman,' he said in the end. 'Since it will bring you consolation, I shall not refuse you. And may it be God's will that in this sanctuary, where you have perhaps never ventured, you find peace for your soul and forgiveness for your sins. Come at nine o'clock, madame, I shall be waiting for you in the sacristy.'

Oh, my dear Jean, what a man that priest was! And how willing the human heart is to deceive itself. Would you believe my suffering seemed to have eased, would you believe I told myself that perhaps all was not lost, that a miracle might be accomplished!

As nine o'clock rang from the little church's bell tower, I arrived, trembling, but in a spirit of pious contemplation, outside the sacristy door where we had agreed to meet. Through the half open doorway I could see in profile the worthy priest's cassock, feebly illuminated by a small lamp. He took it up, and I followed him, grasping two candles, to the underground chamber where the body of my poor Paul lay.

We had come down here, without exchanging a word, into an oppressive silence. And after having received, from the priest's hand, the holy water, I threw myself on my knees, whilst he, blessing those dear mortal remains, said a short prayer. Then vaguely, as in a dream, I heard him murmur, 'Courage'. And the sound of his footsteps echoed under the vault...

I was alone, alone with him.

It was as if the world had caved in! It was as if life itself was rent asunder!

At first I felt fear, the fear of a poor woman whose nerves are stretched to their limits.

This silence, this holy place, these walls whose very stones gave the lie to my existence; and then this body, this little body lying there, hands together beneath his shroud. I shivered uncontrollably.

But almost at the same time, a sense of the immense significance of what I had been permitted to do came over me and comforted me.

Tears poured from my eyes, such tears! They flowed as they can never have flowed before at any shrine or beside the body of any loved one. And there, hands shaking, still on my knees, I understood what it meant to know infinite grief.

It is atrocious and it is delicious. How small one feels, how unimportant, as when a storm, breaking over your head, obliterates you entirely!

Pray! Yes, I would have liked to pray, as one does in a shipwreck. But every time I directed my thoughts on high, they slid back to the one who slept down here, over whom I was keeping watch.

So this is what had come to pass: the dream I had cherished all my life ended beside a coffin; the words I had guarded so long in the closeness of my heart were never to be more than an echo in a funeral vault; the secrets that had burned like fires inside me were to be told to a corpse. Yes, I spoke my thoughts out loud, I called to him, I implored him.

'My Paul…! My beloved…! My only love…! My lost darling…! My child! Yes, my child, for I have loved you with every sort of love, as a mother, as a sister, as a lover. This is the end, then, the end; can it be possible? When you take away your life you take away mine as well, and it is to you, the dead you, that the cry rises from my heart: I love you.'

"I love you": imagine saying that in a church, with God right beside you! You must agree, my dear friend, at least it wasn't commonplace.

Now that I am writing these things down, it reminds me of something out of a play by de Musset. But at the time, I had no thought for anything except him and me, the two of us and our poor love.

And around that catafalque, merging into the indeterminate shadows, my thoughts seemed to dance in a ring like ghosts!

I saw him again that day when, with a corner of blue sky above and tender April air all around, he made his burning declaration of love. I remembered my initial transports of rapture at knowing a love so long sought and finally found, and I closed my eyes so as not to see the ruins of all these joys.

But suddenly I heard a slight noise somewhere near me.

I listened, the blood pulsing in my ears and horrible poundings in my heart. What was that? Good God! – Nothing, my dear, no, it was nothing, just one of the candles sputtering.

Yes, yes, the candles were slowly burning down, and their smell now was acrid, pervasive, disturbing. And I realised that the long hours of this night must have passed.

Perhaps it was daylight outside, and the moment for the

last farewell had come.

Already! Time to go already! And to leave him, leave behind me the best thing in my life! All the same, I stood up, broken, as if dead, as if I had died in my turn.

But alas, we sometimes have more strength than is good for us: I did not move away, I stood there, for a long time, a very long time, my eyes fixed on the white cross that stood out against the funeral drapery, caught in the candles' last gleams.

Finally, retreating backwards, my arms reaching out to the one who lay at rest, I found myself close to the door of the crypt. Across the space separating us I sent the last kiss, the kiss he would take with him into the ground, passionate, despairing, made of fire and tears; then, slipping away like a shadow, I left him.

Oh, happiness, elusive phantom! Others, who deserved it less, have been happy.

I, though, have never managed it and the setting for my first night of love was a tomb.

XXVIII

To the Same

And now, my dearest Jean, it is finished. This is the point at which our correspondence ends. I thank you for having made it possible.

I have re-opened for you, at length, these wounds, and you may see that all the later pages seem to be by a different woman from the one who began by telling you some of her stories. So now you know my full history, my whole life to the present day, and I have nothing left to tell you.

Now that you know this past, full of wishes that proved futile and hopes that proved deceptive, do you understand why I am not the joyful Josiane you were expecting to find? And what will the future be?

Oh, dear Jean! All this is not encouraging; and what a lesson to send to those women who believe they have only to stretch out a hand and happiness is there for the taking!

And therefore, for me, the matter is settled. I no longer wish for anything, I shall no longer look for anything, I no longer believe! The days will pass as they may, and the hours however it suits them!

Unless…

Yes, I pause, and here, unsolicited, a thought goes through my mind: unless, disenchanted and battered as I may be, all at once, one day, the thing inside me flowers again, and at the moment when I am least thinking about it, and in spite of myself, I begin again and throw myself once more into the pursuit of the impossible happiness…

And deep down, would you like me to tell you? Would you like to know what I really think, the secret truth?

I am still waiting, still hoping for that day to come. It makes no difference, telling myself I have failed, I have suffered too much. Yes, I will begin again, an irresistible force drives me to hope, in spite of everything, and eternally. In all truth, what better purpose can life have than this search for happiness and love? Nothing here on earth is worth more than a kiss.

Dedalus Celebrating Women's Literature
2018–2028

In 2018 Dedalus began celebrating the centenary of women getting the vote in the UK with a programme of women's fiction. In 1918, Parliament passed an act granting the vote to women over the age of 30 who were householders, the wives of householders, occupiers of property with an annual rent of £5 or graduates of British universities. About 8.4 million women gained the vote. It was a big step forward but it was not until the Equal Franchise Act of 1928 that women over 21 were able to vote and women finally achieved the same voting rights as men. This act increased the number of women eligible to vote to 15 million. Dedalus' aim is to publish 6 titles each year, most of which will be translations from other European languages, for the next 10 years as we commemorate this important milestone.

Titles published so far:

The Prepper Room by Karen Duve
Take Six: Six Portuguese Women Writers edited by Margaret Jull Costa
Slav Sisters: The Dedalus Book of Russian Women's Literature edited by Natasha Perova
Baltic Belles: The Dedalus Book of Estonian Women's Literature edited by Elle-Mari Talivee
The Madwoman of Serrano by Dina Salústio
Cleopatra goes to Prison by Claudia Durastanti

The Price of Dreams by Margherita Giacobino
Primordial Soup by Christine Leunens
The Girl from the Sea and other Stories by Sophia de Mello
Breyner Andresen
The Medusa Child by Sylvie Germain
Venice Noir by Isabella Panfido
Chasing the Dream by Liane de Pougy
A Woman's Affair by Liane de Pougy

Forthcoming titles include:

Baltic Belles: The Dedalus Book of Latvian Women's Literature
edited by Eva Eglaja
Fair Trade Heroin by Rachael McGill
Co-Wives, Co-Widows by Adrienne Yabouza
Catalogue of a Private Life by Najwa Binshatwan
Eddo's Souls by Stella Gaitano

For further information please contact Dedalus at
info@dedalusbooks.com

A Woman's Affair – Liane de Pougy

A Woman's Affair (*Idylle Saphique*) published in 1901, shocked
French readers with its lesbian lover story which was based on
Liane de Pougy's affair with Natalie Barney. Today it is seen
as a *fin-de-siècle* classic.

Despite her beauty and her riches, Annhine de Lys, one of the
most notorious courtesans of 1890s Paris, is bored and restless.
Into her life bursts Flossie, a young American woman, and
everything changes. The love she offers Annhine is dangerous,
perverse and hard to resist. Ignoring the warnings of her best
friend, Annhine encourages the affair. Yet she cannot commit:
she advances, retreats, becomes bewildered, ill. After a tragic
incident at a masked ball, Annhine leaves Paris to make a long
tour through Europe. But the attempt to put time and distance
between them comes to nothing and the fateful relationship
must run its course.

£9.99   ISBN 978 1 912868 48 3   314p   B. Format